"Hasn't anyone ever given you flowers?"

His lips turned up with pleasure and a hint of amusement. "Not that I recall. I'd even forgotten how wonderful they smell. Thank you, Paula."

She smiled up at him in the sunshine shimmering through the eucalyptus trees, and it seemed that the two of them were encircled by the fragrance of roses. She was uncertain why she'd brought them; perhaps it was to learn whether he still had the same bittersweet effect on her as when she was a girl.

"Would you like to come in?" he asked. "Maybe you can help locate a vase. I don't remember where Mom keeps things anymore."

"Up there, if I remember correctly." Paula pointed to a high cabinet over the kitchen sink.

Matt carried over a rickety stepstool. "Seems like I did get vases out of there for Mom."

As he climbed the first two steps, Paula was aware of the strength in his tan arms; they were covered with blond curly hair. She forced her eyes back to the cabinet.

"The door's stuck." He tugged mightily on the cut-glass knob, and the cabinet door flew open. Below him, the stool jerked, throwing him off balance.

"Oh!" she called out, reaching up to steady him.

The stool crashed down behind him, and Matt fell against her upraised arms. For an instant his arms tightened around her as he caught his balance. The weight of his body against hers and his clean soapy smell made her senses reel. He moved away, taking hold of her shoulders. "I'm sorry! I hope I didn't hurt you."

Echoes of Love

ELAINE SCHULTE

Serenade/Serenata
BOOKS
of the Zondervan Publishing House
Grand Rapids, Michigan

A Note from the Author: *I love to hear from my readers! You may correspond with me by writing:*

Elaine Schulte
Author Relations
1415 Lake Drive, S.E.
Grand Rapids, MI 49506

ECHOES OF LOVE
Copyright © 1986 by Elaine Schulte

Serenade/Serenata is an imprint of Zondervan Publishing House, 1415 Lake Drive, S.E., Grand Rapids, Michigan 49506.

ISBN 0-310-47221-0

With special appreciation to Deloris Isbister
and Aileen Henderson

Edited by Sandra L. Vander Zicht
Designed by Kim Koning

Printed in the United States of America

86 87 88 89 90 91 92 / 10 9 8 7 6 5 4 3 2 1

To Jackie and Bob Matthew with love

*Our echoes roll from soul to soul,
and grow for ever and for ever. . . .*

Tennyson
"The Splendor Falls"
Songs of the Princess

chapter
1

THROUGH THE DARKNESS OF SLEEP, Paula heard ringing. Time to wake up, she thought, though it didn't sound like her raucous alarm clock. Blinking groggily, she leaned across the bed and pressed in the clock's alarm button, confused by the strangely familiar peach-colored walls, the Victorian furniture. Of course—she was home. Not in her tiny condo in Phoenix but really home—upstairs in her parents' venerable Spanish house in Southern California.

She peered at her old ivory clock. Eleven-thirty. The morning was nearly gone, but then she hadn't arrived until 2:00 A.M.

Unpleasant memories assailed the edges of her consciousness, and she forced them away, not wanting to remember the heartbreaking details of why she'd run home. It was terrible enough to recall that she'd entrusted a man with her heart and her hopes, and now, because of his lies, she'd have to decide what to do with her life.

Perhaps she could sleep longer, just another fifteen minutes. She was too exhausted to make up her mind about anything yet.

Lying back on the cool pillow, she remembered her parents had mentioned Matt Montgomery last night. How strange that she'd nearly forgotten about him lately. Did they assume he'd help her overcome her heartbreak? Or that she'd go on the Yucatan trip since he was going?

She reset the alarm to ring in fifteen minutes, then rolled over and pulled the light bedsheet over her shoulders, drowsily welcoming the grayness again.

Matt Montgomery . . . She remembered bringing him an armful of roses. Of all the simple-minded things—taking him an armful of roses! But she'd been twenty-one then. It was nearly two years ago when she'd been home from college for spring vacation and Matt was visiting his parents next door. On Saturday morning, she'd impulsively cut roses from the garden for him. She could still visualize him as she drifted off to sleep.

She rang the Montgomerys' front doorbell with wavering courage. At the sound of its melodious chimes inside, she nearly fled, but already firm footsteps approached the door.

Matt opened it, a slow smile spreading across his face. "Well, look who's here—Paula Ingraham!" He wore a pale blue knit shirt and tan slacks, and towered above her in the doorway.

"Hi, Matt," she responded with an awkward catch in her throat. He was even more attractive than she remembered: sun-streaked blond hair, dazzling smile, and deep rift in his chin. How mature he looked now. It wasn't just his broad shoulders and solid stance; it was the determination in his blue eyes.

Nervously she thrust the flowers toward him, shades of red, yellow, pink, and white all jumbled together. "A homecoming present."

He gazed at the bouquet in astonishment. "For *me?*"

"Hasn't anyone ever given you flowers?" she inquired as if it were a natural gesture on her part.

His lips turned up with pleasure and a hint of amusement. "Not that I recall. I'd even forgotten how wonderful they smell. Thank you, Paula."

She smiled up at him in the sunshine shimmering through the eucalyptus trees, and it seemed that the two of them were encircled by the fragrance of roses. She was uncertain why she'd brought them; perhaps it was to learn whether he still had the same bittersweet effect on her as when she was a girl.

His eyes darted to her short tennis dress and widened. "I'm certain that I've never received flowers from anyone so beautiful."

She laughed lightly, not believing him. Her figure was slim, and perhaps she was pretty with her honey-blond hair and blue-green eyes, but she was not beautiful. Her smile was her best feature, she supposed, her teeth having been in braces for four long years.

"Would you like to come in?" he asked. "Maybe you can help locate a vase."

She followed him through the familiar hallway to the pale yellow kitchen where years ago she had eaten his mother's freshly baked chocolate chip cookies. This morning, the aromas of coffee and bacon still lingered.

"Mom and Dad are out," Matt explained, placing the roses on the old stainless drainboard.

Heat rushed to her cheeks, and she was thankful his attention was directed toward the kitchen cabinets. She'd known very well that his parents were gone; they'd left before she cut the roses!

"I don't remember where Mom keeps things anymore," he remarked, banging open one cabinet after another in search of a vase.

"Up there, if I remember correctly." Paula pointed to a high cabinet over the kitchen sink. "They're with the big punch bowl we've borrowed for special occasions."

Matt carried over a rickety stepstool. "Seems like I did get vases out of there for Mom."

As he climbed the first two steps, Paula was aware of the strength in his tan arms; they were covered with blond curly hair. She forced her eyes back to the cabinet.

"The door's stuck." He tugged mightily on the cut-glass knob, and the cabinet door flew open. Below him, the stool jerked, throwing him off balance.

"Oh!" she called out, reaching up to steady him.

The stool crashed down behind him, and Matt fell against her upraised arms. For an instant his arms tightened around her as he caught his balance. The weight of his body against hers and his clean soapy smell made her senses reel. He moved away, taking hold of her shoulders. "I'm sorry! I hope I didn't hurt you."

She shook her head and forced herself away. If only he knew that her fondest wish years ago had been to be in his arms!

"Are you sure you're all right?" he asked.

"Yes, just fine," she replied, although her heart pounded wildly.

He laughed and righted the stool. "Well, let's give it another try."

"I'll hold it," she offered and steadied the stool as he climbed up again.

He located a brass vase. "I hope this will do."

"Yes, it's lovely—"

"You'll have to give me a hand with the roses." His deep voice was calm as if he'd already dismissed their being in each others' arms. "Flower Arranging is one class I never took."

"Nor I," she returned as evenly as possible.

At length they chatted about the neighborhood news, then their own lives as they arranged the roses in the vase. Finally he carried them to the living room and set them down on the oak coffee table. "I can't believe you'll soon graduate from college." Looking at her oddly, he said, "There's a good movie on downtown tonight. Would you like to go?"

She managed a restrained, "Yes, thank you. I'd enjoy that, Matt."

She'd scarcely been able to contain her excitement all day.

When he picked her up in the evening, he already seemed distant. In the darkened theater, she placed her hand on the armrest between them, desperately hoping that he might hold it. Please, Matt, please love me, she thought.

He seemed oblivious to her availability. Once when she reached for their popcorn, she caught him watching her, but he merely smiled and turned away to the movie. He probably still sees me as a child, she thought, and the warm popcorn stuck in her throat. Sadly, the evening did not improve.

At her parents' front door, the porch light turned his face into shadows and sharply etched planes. "It was good seeing you again after all these years, Paula." His tone rang with finality.

She put on a bright smile. "Yes . . . well, thanks for the movie."

"I'm flying back to Sunnyvale tomorrow night," he said as if to reemphasize the end of their relationship. Perhaps it was only the light, but his face appeared grim with determination, as though he knew just where he was and where he was going, and there was no room for her in his plan. He made no move toward her, not even to shake her hand.

She unlocked the door quickly. "Thanks again, Matt. See you."

Her smile faded the instant she closed the door. Oh, Matt! her heart cried out, Why is it that I've always loved you so, and you've always seen me as the little girl next door?

When the alarm clock rang again, Paula awoke with a start. She'd been dreaming! She reflected over what a childish dream it had always been, though the roses and their so-called date had been real enough. She had agonized again and again over her stupidity in bringing him roses—and now to have dreamed of it too.

Rumor had it that Matt, once the neighborhood Eagle Scout, had turned into a playboy, dating one beautiful woman after another. As president of an electronics company, he had undoubtedly showered his dates with roses . . . and not of the homegrown variety. Enough about him! she decided, sitting up in bed. Now she needed to find a job and an apartment. And today was the final day to make reservations for the Yucatan trip, *if* she decided to go. She swung her slim legs to the floor and stood up on the thick white carpeting.

Gayle, her dearest friend, would stop by for lunch in half an hour. She'd undoubtedly be as brimful of excitement as was the note she'd typed on her mother's Santa Rosita Travel Agency letterhead three months ago. Paula extracted it from her handbag and read the note again.

It began humorously enough with *Dear Fellow Archeologist, Paula*—humorous because she'd attended only a few archeology seminars with Gayle in college, and they'd dug together at a prehistoric Indian site in New Mexico with Gayle's favorite professor and other archeology buffs.

> Great, great news! I've dug out the old Santa Rosita High and City College yearbooks to get a group together for a two-week tour of the Yucatan in February. It's going to be a dream come true! Let's be roommates again!
>
> Your old roomie,
Gayle
>
> P.S. Matt Montgomery has signed up!

Surely Gayle means this as an added enticement, Paula thought when the letter had arrived in Phoenix. But Matt hadn't mattered then! She'd fallen in love with Tony Rilki, owner of the public relations firm where she worked, and he was in the process of getting a divorce so he could marry her. She still hadn't discovered his deceitfulness when she'd replied to Gayle, with a "Thanks, but no thanks, old roomie. Would you believe I'm in love!"

Now that she'd fled Tony, given up her job and Phoenix apartment, and returned to Santa Rosita, Gayle would probably try again to convince her to go on the Yucatan tour. During these last weeks of upheaval, her mother had mentioned the trip on the phone. And now it was only a week away. How life had changed in three months!

She remembered arriving home last night, and her parents happily climbing out of bed to welcome her. "How exhausted you look, Paula." Her trim mother, so lovely with her halo of salt-and-pepper curls, had looked older somehow; her father appeared grayer too. They'd sat sleepily with her at the kitchen table while she sipped steaming hot chocolate, feeling loved and pampered—an only child again.

"I am tired," Paula admitted. "I suppose I shouldn't have tried moving and driving home all in one day."

"After all that you've been through, you should rest this week and then get away," her mother suggested. "You need new surroundings. Gayle said there were still openings on the Yucatan trip when I called to invite her to lunch tomorrow. I hope that's all right, inviting her to lunch."

"It's more than all right. I've missed her too."

Her mother added, "Think about the trip."

"I don't know. At the moment I doubt I'll have the energy to go anywhere except to bed for weeks."

Her father said, "I'll spring for a jungle outfit for pyramid climbing."

Ordinarily she'd grab at the chance to go, but not now.

"Matt Montgomery is going," her father added.

Paula glanced sharply at him, but she saw he'd merely stated a fact. Matt was going. That was all. The last thing she needed was another man, especially someone like Matt. He would only remind her of her knack for falling in love with the wrong men.

Her mother laughed. "It's hard to believe that Matt used to babysit you."

"Yes, I suppose it is," Paula agreed. Their so-called romance had been hopeless from the start. She'd been eight years old, and he'd been fifteen—her babysitter! Her family had just moved to Santa Rosita, and she'd peered warily from behind the living room draperies to see this Matt Montgomery.

The instant he stepped from the front door of his house, she was stunned. He was wonderfully handsome . . . and in high school.

She had answered the door herself.

"Are you Paula?" he inquired.

His deep blue eyes held hers, and finally she nodded. She had never forgotten that moment. Shortly thereafter, she gave up braids and arranged her hair a hundred different ways, trying to attract his attention. She and Gayle ran behind him while he delivered newspapers on his bike.

"What are you kids up to?" he'd call back while he pedaled along. But he didn't seem to care, for he continued to pursue Vanessa Starke, the most gorgeous girl in the high school.

When he left for Stanford University, Paula tried to forget him, but he constantly invaded her daydreams, especially when Vanessa married someone else. After five years of college, Matt remained in Northern California, moving to

16

Sunnyvale. He was so preoccupied with starting and then running a high-tech company that he rarely came home.

The seven years between them always seemed insurmountable. But now she was twenty-three and Matt was thirty. Perhaps he'd see her differently on a trip, she speculated before realizing that she was still daydreaming about him.

As she and her parents headed upstairs last night she'd said, "I think I'd better start job hunting Monday instead of gallivanting around Mayan ruins."

They looked disappointed, and she quickly added, "Can you put up with me at home again until I find an apartment?"

"You're welcome as long as you please," they responded.

Her mother had kissed her cheek, adding, "Isn't it curious that Matt should be staying with his parents next door now? He's househunting in Santa Rosita. He'll be moving back since he's sold his company."

Paula had cast a suspicious glance at her too, but her mother apparently was only sharing an item of neighborhood interest. Fond as they'd been of Matt, her parents had always discouraged her crush on him, pointing out the seven-year difference in their ages.

How odd to have fallen asleep thinking about him last night, then this morning to have dreamed about the roses. For a while, at least, she had forgotten Tony.

She'd have to hurry to shower. As she passed her Victorian chest of drawers, she noticed the framed photograph of herself with Gayle, striding along arm-in-arm in front of Santa Rosita High and smiling as if they owned the sun, the moon, and the stars.

Well, she certainly hadn't felt like that lately, Paula thought, though she wasn't ready to give up on life yet.

Half an hour later, she hurried downstairs in tan slacks topped by a tan-and-white-striped sweater. Inspecting herself in the entry mirror, she was pleased at how refreshed she appeared for the first time in weeks. It's from being home, she thought, from sleeping well at last after the break-up with Tony. Thank goodness I asked Mother to tell Gayle about it.

The smell of warm blueberry muffins lured her to the kitchen, where she found them cooling. A note taped on the refrigerator handle read,

> Forgot to tell you it's my volunteer day at the hospital. Salad and blueberry muffins for you and Gayle. Ice cream in the freezer if you want dessert.

> Love, Mother

Paula found the salad in the refrigerator and took out butter to soften. How like her mother to have invited Gayle for lunch and to have baked muffins this morning. The house was polished up too. The kitchen's Mexican tile floor gleamed, as did the copper pots and pans hanging over the work center. Near the French doors, the round oak table held a basket brimming with red-orange tangelos—undoubtedly part of the backyard tree's usual bumper crop.

Outside, the sun beamed through the overhanging pepper tree and onto the brick patio. She opened the door, and the mild Santa Ana breeze greeted her warmly. Despite it being early February, they could eat lunch on the patio.

Paula heard high heels clicking faintly. Then Gayle hurried around the side of the house, her upswept red curls shining in the sunlight. She looked marvelous as usual, wearing a navy blazer over a kelly green dress.

"Paula . . ." Gayle's elfin face curved into a cautious smile, but her enormous green eyes brimmed with concern. "I thought you'd be back here! You look . . . just fine. I didn't know what to expect . . ."

To Paula's astonishment, her lips began to quiver, and a soft sob escaped her as she rushed into Gayle Oliver's arms.

"Oh, honey," Gayle said, holding her close. "You're home. Everything's going to be all right now. It's really going to be fine. If only you weren't so trusting."

"But you are too!" Paula returned.

"You trusted the wrong person—"

Paula pulled away, her lashes moist. "I know. And, worst of all, Tony always said, 'Trust your friends today as if they'll be your enemies tomorrow.' Why didn't I understand I shouldn't have trusted him?"

"I suppose you didn't want to," Gayle responded. "Still, it's better to be hurt occasionally than *never* to trust."

"I don't know . . . it's too dangerous to trust!" She was appalled at the hot tears that burst from her eyes, and it took a moment to bring her emotions under control. "It leaves us too vulnerable." She wiped her eyes. "I'm sorry. You're the first person to see me cry about this."

"You must have needed it." Gayle fumbled for a tissue in her handbag. "Oh, how I'd like to give that Tony a good shaking!"

"A good shaking he could use," Paula said. "But *you?*"

Gayle bristled as she handed over a tissue. "At the very least, I'd give him a good talking to!"

"He could use that as well, although I can't imagine what good it'd do." Paula mustered a smile. "I think I'm finished crying."

"You want to talk about it?" Gayle asked quietly.

"Suffice it to say that Tony lied about being in the midst of a divorce. Moreover, he neglected to mention that there'd been a prior marriage and two children in Chicago!"

Gayle shook her head. "I can't believe it!"

"I couldn't either, at first. At any rate, his second wife has money, and he'd never abandon that for me." She shrugged hopelessly. "He loved me in his own way, I suppose. He's the kind of a man who needs the drama of two women in his life. I wasn't his first *other* woman and probably won't be his last."

"At least you didn't waste your entire life on him!" Gayle replied. "Some women do on men like that."

"But I should have known better! He blamed the entire impasse on me for being so darn . . . virginal. I'm still not quite sure why I held out. . . ."

"Thank goodness you did!" Gayle responded with vehemence. "If you hadn't, you'd have that guilt to deal with too . . . and who knows what else! Just give it all up to the Lord, honey."

Paula was in no mood to contemplate that.

"Let's get down to business and eat that lunch your mother promised," Gayle suggested. "You're looking far too thin."

By the time the salad was tossed and they were outside eating, Gayle maneuvered the conversation to the Yucatan trip. "You have to go, Paula," she insisted, spearing a bit of tomato with her fork. "It's the chance of a lifetime! Moreover, I've talked Dr. Zayere into speaking at our pretrip meeting next week."

"How did you pull off that?" Dr. Zayere had conducted the seminars on archeology she'd occasionally attended with Gayle during their last two years at the university. And last June after graduation, he'd headed the archeological dig in New Mexico.

"Things just seemed to fall into place," Gayle said.

"Things always fall into place for you," Paula responded with a shake of her head. "And I tried to talk you out of minoring in archeology!" As it turned out, Gayle's business-and-archeology background had become quite useful—far more useful than her own degree in journalism.

"Come with us," Gayle pleaded.

"I'll think about it," Paula answered, biting into a warm blueberry muffin.

"Would it help to remind you Matt Montgomery is going?"

Paula glanced toward the Montgomery house, most of which was hidden by eucalyptus trees and a wooden fence covered with bougainvillaea. "That bit of information won't entice me."

"What about our being roommates again?"

"That might," Paula admitted with a smile. "But at the moment I have to find a new job and an apartment."

When they relaxed after lunch, she noted something different about Gayle, an excitement dancing in her green eyes. "What's the secret?" Paula asked.

"I'll tell you tomorrow."

"Why not now?" She was suddenly suspicious. "It's not one of your schemes for my snaring Matt?" She remembered some of their harebrained ideas for getting Matt's attention when they were girls. "I'm most definitely not going to roller skate by his house again!"

Gayle laughed. "It has nothing to do with Matt. Trust me. Tomorrow night. Let's have dinner at my house. By the way, Evan Walker is going on the trip, too, along with some of his friends from the computer company where he works. He's divorced now."

"What happened?" Paula asked. Evan had once taken her to a high school prom and a few movies, but their relationship had never been serious.

"His wife forgot the part of the marriage vows about forsaking all others. The marriage was a disaster."

"Poor Evan," Paula sympathized.

When Gayle left for the travel agency at one-thirty, Paula was too tired to unpack the suitcases in her room. Still, she didn't want to go to bed on such a beautiful day. Perhaps she would lie out in the sun by the neighborhood pool.

She slipped into an old white one-piece bathing suit and grabbed her new paperback novel and dark glasses. After locking up the house, she headed through the backyard toward the pool complex. No one will be around on a February afternoon, she thought as she approached the ivy-covered wall surrounding the pool.

She opened the squeaking redwood gate and started for the sunny side of the pool deck, aware only of the warm breeze rustling the ivy and the palm trees.

"Paula!" a low male voice called out.

The sound of Matt speaking her name made her catch her breath. She turned and watched him get up from a lounge behind the gate. "Hello, Matt! I didn't dream you'd be here too."

He strode toward her, obviously admiring her trim figure. Her thoughts faltered, then from force of habit she smiled and held her hand out to him.

"You look terrific," he said.

"You too," she answered. There were lines at the corners of his mouth and beneath his blue eyes that she hadn't noticed before.

"Thought I'd get some sun," she said and sat down more quickly than she anticipated on the nearest chaise lounge.

"Doesn't the sun shine in Phoenix nowadays?" he asked amiably, settling on the lounge next to hers.

She laughed. "I haven't had time to find out lately." During the last few weeks in Phoenix, it seemed as if she were living under a dark cloud.

"Working too hard?" he asked.

"I quit my job. I'm moving back to Santa Rosita."

"You too?"

She nodded. "Mom told me that you're househunting—that you've sold your company, but I don't know the details."

"I sold it to a conglomerate."

"Congratulations!"

"Thanks, but it's less than an unqualified success."

"I don't understand."

Matt shrugged. "Despite the conglomerate's promises, I found I was no longer in a position to steer the company."

"Bad attorney?"

He shook his head. "Afraid it was my own fault. I'd pushed myself to the point of exhaustion, to the point of wanting to trust someone else's promises. They'd given in to all of my major demands so I was inclined to be a little too trusting." He sighed with resignation. "Actually it worked out according to my original plan . . . founding a company and selling it in five to seven years."

"I suppose that's what's important," she said. He didn't look especially pleased with the millions he might have made from selling his company. She glanced up and found his blue eyes studying her, no doubt still seeing the little nuisance next door.

The soft breeze ruffled his hair. "I saw Gayle arriving at your house," he said, sitting back on the lounge. "I guess you know the big news."

"Big news?"

"About her and Josh being engaged."

"Gayle and Josh Granville?" She could scarcely believe it, although they'd been dating since last summer. Josh had been Matt's best friend all through school. When Matt had run for class office and student council president, Josh had been his biggest booster; shy as he was, Josh had always managed winning campaigns for Matt.

Matt raised a surprised brow. "She didn't tell you?"

"No, not yet," Paula answered, puzzled, "but she was saving a secret for tomorrow." It would be like Gayle not to mention her wonderful news in the face of someone else's distress.

"I was certain she would have said something," Matt said in dismay. "You two were always best friends."

Paula looked away toward the diving board. "We discussed other things."

"Look, I really am sorry."

"It's okay, Matt," she reassured him. "I'll pretend to be wildly surprised."

"Thanks."

He looked so embarrassed that she cast about for another topic. "I hear that you're going on the Yucatan trip."

"Yes. Josh and I are going to be roommates. Gayle said that she was going to try to talk you into it." He laughed. "You *do* know about that?"

"Yes, that I know."

His blue eyes turned serious. "I hope you're going."

Her heart suddenly beat faster. "Yes," she found herself saying. "Yes, I'm going. I'm . . . looking forward to it."

"Wonderful!" He glanced at his watch and sat up with a start. "I'm late for a meeting," he said, getting to his feet. "Thanks for not telling Gayle that I gave the news away."

"Sure, Matt."

"See you, Paula."

She sat on the chaise in shock. It was surprising enough that Gayle was going to marry Josh Granville, but even more astonishing that she . . . that Paula Marie Ingraham was going to the Yucatan. It would clean out most of her savings, and she hadn't planned . . .

Matt waved to her as he retrieved a tailored white beach jacket from a chaise by the gate.

Still astonished, she could only wave back.

It was a while before she reminded herself that he'd sold his company and that his meeting was probably more pleasure than business . . . and most likely business with a beautiful woman!

chapter
2

PAULA WAS UNPACKING HER SUITCASES and cartons the next morning when Tom Timmons, editor of the biweekly *Santa Rosita Times*, telephoned. "I heard you're going to the Yucatan," he said. "How about writing two or three freelance travel articles for us? There's such a big group going from Santa Rosita."

She was speechless. She had worked there as a summer intern while in college, but she'd written mostly community news and obituaries. "Thanks, but I've never—"

"I've got a tip sheet on writing travel articles for you."

"The only thing I've ever written that's remotely similar was that series on local parks and historic areas."

"You did a good job," he said, surprising her further. Tom Timmons was more apt to criticize than to praise.

"We can't pay much," he continued, "but I have a list of ten or twelve biweeklies and weeklies in other circulation areas. You can probably resell the articles to them if you do a good job—a little self-syndication. Are you game?"

"I'll be right over." After all, she did have a degree in journalism, Paula thought, though she'd made little use of it so far. Surely she could write the articles. Most likely, there was no one else to write them for the *Santa Rosita Times* anyhow.

She ran a comb through her hair and grabbed her handbag, pausing in the kitchen to tell her mother about the phone call.

"How would Tom Timmons know?" her mother asked, looking up from making potato salad at the kitchen table.

"I suppose Gayle mentioned it. I called her last night to say I was going on the trip."

"Maybe an exciting job will come of your doing the articles."

"Maybe," Paula answered with a laugh, then kissed the top of her mother's head before hurrying out.

Climbing into her white Cutlass, she realized that her spirits had lifted since she'd decided to go on the trip. Perhaps those who said the best way to forget heartbreak was to run away were right. At any rate, the Yucatan's ancient Mayan civilization would serve as an excellent preoccupation.

At the old downtown *Times* office, she noted that little had changed: the same scarred yellow oak desks, familiar stacks of files, and paperwork everywhere. Tom Timmons looked as harried as usual, even for a Saturday morning, his thatch of gray hair as wild as ever, his paunch a trifle larger.

"You'll do a good job, Paula." He handed over the tip sheet and the list of newspapers to which she might resell rights. "You've always been conscientious, always will be. Just give us lots of people interest . . . the ancient and contemporary Mayans, maybe a little on the Spanish conquistadors. Not the people in the Santa Rosita tour group. We don't want a society piece."

He hurried to a nearby cubicle and emerged with rolls of film. "Here's a dozen rolls. We'll develop them for you."

Still amazed, Paula could only shake her head and smile as she watched him stuff the film into a crumpled old lunch bag from his desk drawer. "I'll do my best," she promised.

"If you have any trouble handling both note-taking and

28

photography, don't forget that Matt Montgomery used to get decent pictures for us when he was in high school. Tell him I'll up the price from five to ten dollars for each picture we print."

"I'll tell him." She repressed a laugh. The last thing Matt needed now was ten dollars a picture!

When she returned home, her mother had a message for her. "Gayle called. She said you should wear something pretty and that Matt will pick you up at seven."

"Matt?"

"Yes. She said it would be you and Matt, and her and Josh for dinner."

"That's the first I've heard of it!" She'd thought that she and Gayle would be alone, sending out for a pizza like old times.

"You didn't know?"

Paula shook her head. Probably the dinner was Gayle's way of breaking the news of her engagement to Josh. She had invited Matt to buffer the impact of her and Josh's joy—to keep memories of Tony at bay. "It sounds like it's all arranged," she said.

Her mother looked at her uneasily. "There's something bothering me about it, Paula."

"What?" It wasn't like her mother to interfere.

"Matt," she replied hesitantly. "I don't want you to be hurt again, and I know you used to idolize him. And . . . well . . . the fact of the matter is that his mother confided something unsettling." She stopped as if to reassess whether to continue.

"What's that?" Paula prompted.

Her mother shrugged with resignation. "It's just that . . . well, he was such a nice boy, but now he does have a reputation with women. His mother said he's turned into a playboy. She thinks it's his way of dealing with Vanessa's rejection."

"Mrs. Montgomery thinks that's *still* bothering him? That was ten years ago!"

Her mother nodded unhappily. "She's deeply upset about it. Anyhow, I wouldn't take him too seriously if I were you, dear."

"I have no intention of taking him or any other man seriously," Paula stated flatly. "That's the very last thing I'd need now."

"What about Evan Walker?" her mother asked. "You said he was going. I've always thought he was nice."

"He is," Paula replied thoughtfully. "It's just that no sparks ever ignited between us."

"Perhaps you were too young."

When Paula returned to her room to finish unpacking, she was determined to stop thinking about men. She concentrated on choosing a dress for the evening and on thinking about researching the travel articles at the library next week. This afternoon she'd study the travel brochures Gayle had given her so she could at least talk intelligently about the Yucatan tonight. Whatever she did, she would not upset herself and mar Gayle's happiness by brooding over Tony.

She eyed the partially unpacked suitcases and boxes on her bed. After an instant's deliberation, she whisked out the new winter white wool dress she'd bought in Phoenix at the after-Christmas sales.

Shaking out the wrinkles, she hung the dress on a satin hanger. It would be perfect with its soft scarf at the neckline, long sleeves, and slightly flared skirt. Moreover, she would feel comfortable wearing the dress since she'd never worn it with Tony. It held no unpleasant memories.

At precisely seven o'clock the doorbell rang, and Paula hurried to answer it in a flurry of nerves.

Matt stood smiling at the door. "You look lovely, Paula," he said, his low voice lingering on her name.

"Thank you, Matt." She did feel lovely wearing the dress, and in the mirror she'd noticed that the off-white color enhanced the golden highlights in her hair and the blue-green of her eyes. "You look nice yourself."

Nice was an understatement. He was very attractive in a navy blazer and gray slacks. His pale blue shirt and the varied shades of blue in his striped necktie heightened the deep blue of his eyes. His sun-burnished blond hair was slightly brushed to the side—the only possible frame for his firm, square face—but a strand had fallen slightly forward, and she had to resist the impulse to reach up and brush it back for him. Everything about him looked perfect and was complemented by a musky cologne.

In the living room, her parents eyed him suspiciously, as if torn between his Eagle Scout days and his playboy reputation. She nearly laughed, for they looked as fiercely protective as when she'd gone on her first date.

If Matt noticed their uneasiness, he ignored it, chatting pleasantly about his search for a house in Santa Rosita Hills or a condo on the beach. He seemed uncertain of the life he wanted to lead now that he had sold his company.

As he helped her into her blue velvet jacket, her mother said, "Have a nice time," but her eyes sought Paula's in warning: *Don't get hurt again!*

Outside, Matt opened the passenger door of his pale blue Porsche. "I thought you might prefer to ride," he said.

"I could hardly resist riding in this!" she replied, though it did seem a trifle odd not to walk since Gayle lived less than a block away. A sudden thought struck her: Do women more readily succumb to his charm in a sports car?

As he slid into the driver's seat, she was intensely aware of him and caught him glancing at her. "I thought you might break a heel or twist your ankle if we walked in the dark," he explained.

"Thank you for your concern," she replied, "but I'm not as helpless as I might look."

He laughed lightly as he backed the car out of the driveway. "Women are seldom as helpless as they pretend to be."

She repressed the retort that came to mind: Some men aren't what they pretend to be either! Instead, she stared into the darkness.

"Sorry. That was an uncalled-for remark," he said into the silence.

"Yes," she replied with a smile, "it was."

"I'll do better," he promised.

It occurred to her that he might feel resentment toward women just as, since Tony, she had been harboring bitterness toward men. Yet it seemed unlikely that Matt would still be bitter about Vanessa Starke's throwing him over for Kurt Packard, an older man with money. Matt had been a student at Stanford then, and Vanessa had just finished her first year at a prestigious women's college back East. However, that might explain why he'd pursued work and wealth so relentlessly.

"Thanks for promising not to tell Gayle that I let out the big news," Matt said. "I wouldn't want to spoil anything for her or Josh."

"I'll pretend it's the surprise of the century," she assured him again. "Actually it is amazing . . . Gayle and Josh Granville."

"They seem very happy."

"Good." She glanced at him, far too aware of the confined intimacy of his sports car. When she was a teenager, she would have given anything to have been in the same car with him. Now she wasn't certain how she felt, only that she must not let herself be too attracted to him.

"Here we are," he said, driving into Gayle's driveway.

As he helped her out of the car, she mused aloud, "Strange that we're all back at home right now."

"Like children," he laughed. "Not that it doesn't have great compensations like decent meals and laundry service."

"And love." Paula remembered how fond Matt's parents had always been of him, then recalled what his mother had said about his being a playboy. Still, she supposed that his mother loved him and that he loved his parents too. "Maybe Gayle's been the smart one all along, living at home."

"Josh says they give each other plenty of breathing space. Her mother and grandmother will no doubt be out tonight."

Matt rang the doorbell of the Olivers' two-story Tudor house, and in moments, Gayle answered, resplendent in a jade dress. "What timely guests!" Her green eyes danced with excitement. "I'm so glad you're here."

Josh joined them in the entry, casually elegant in his tan herringbone sports coat and tan slacks. "Good to see you again, Paula," he said with a glimmer in his eyes.

"It must be at least five years," she said as they shook hands. How he had changed! Instead of the gangly, serious high school boy who'd been Matt's best friend, Josh had matured considerably. Fortunately, his old comical lopsided grin remained.

As they made small talk, Paula realized that Josh had not only become more attractive, but also self-confident and exceedingly happy. He no longer resembled the shy, insecure boy whom everyone thought couldn't possibly live up to his parents' images as pillars of the community or make his way in their prestigious law firm.

While he hung Paula's jacket in the entry closet, she turned to Gayle. With her gamine features she had never been a raving beauty, but she looked radiantly beautiful now.

"Would you believe that Josh is helping me cook dinner?" Gayle asked as they stepped into the oak-paneled living room.

"Josh cooking!" Matt exclaimed. "This I have to see."

"Now, Matt," Josh protested. "Not only am I a budding chef, but we're considering a cooking class in France while we're on our honeymoon. . . ."

Gayle shook her head. "Oh, Josh, you've given it away!"

Josh rolled his eyes skyward. "I did it."

Matt patted his back. "Better you than me, old man." His blue eyes darted to Paula.

"What's all this?" she asked innocently.

Gayle slipped her hand almost shyly into Josh's. "We're engaged," she said, beaming. "And on top of that, we're getting married!"

"Oh, Gayle . . . !" Paula hugged her. "That's the most wonderful news! I'm so happy for you!" She *was,* she thought. The tears blurring her eyes were happiness for Gayle.

"How about me?" Josh asked, and Paula reached up to kiss his cheek.

"Oh, you'd better be good to my best friend!" she warned him half-jokingly.

"I will," Josh promised with his familiar lopsided grin. "Don't worry, I will." He slipped an arm proudly around Gayle's shoulder.

Paula examined the two of them together. Despite nearly ten inches of difference in height, they looked a perfect match, and so in love that they seemed to radiate joy. "I want to fix this sight in my memory," she said.

Matt shook his head hopelessly. "These two lovebirds are to be our roommates on the trip!"

Paula laughed. "I don't think we'll be seeing a whole lot of them."

As they sat down on the curved white living room couch, Gayle said, "Paula, I hope you'll be my maid of honor for the wedding."

"I can't think of anything I'd rather do!" Paula exclaimed, rushing to hug her friend again.

"I don't know," Josh remarked, "Matt didn't react like that when I asked him to be my best man."

They all laughed, and Paula tried to hide her momentary surprise. There was really nothing astonishing about Matt's being the best man—it was just that once again they would be thrown together.

Gayle jumped up. "I'm going to burn the dinner! Excuse me!"

"We'll give you a hand," Matt said, and they all trailed happily behind Gayle.

The spacious old kitchen was redolent with the tantalizing smells of French onion soup and *boeuf bourguignon*. Paula, set to work stirring the aromatic beef stew, was surprised to see that Matt knew how to cook the homemade noodles.

When they carried the hot dishes into the Tudor-beamed dining room, a fire crackled in the huge fireplace, and romantic music surrounded them. Lighting the candles on the table, Paula looked up and found Matt watching her intently. She quickly dropped her eyes. He probably assumed that Gayle had set up this romantic dinner to ensnare them too.

"It looks like you two are marvelous cooks," she said to Gayle and Josh as they all sat down for dinner. There were brown pottery bowls of French onion soup still bubbling under thick golden crusts of cheese accompanied by long crusty French bread and rich butter.

"Josh came by last night to help me start the dinner."

"We used nearly every pot in the kitchen," he laughed.

Matt chuckled. "I can't believe you're becoming so domestic."

"You haven't seen anything yet!" Josh retorted. "We're going to buy a house out in the country and fill it with flowers and cats and dogs and . . ." He turned to Gayle.

"And lots of children," she added with a blush.

"Oh, Gayle," Paula sighed. "I'm so very happy for you." She felt a twinge of envy, then reminded herself that there was no point in yearning for what she would probably never have—a house, a husband, two or three darling children, and love filling every corner of her life. She had dreamed of that with Tony, and he had hedged so cleverly. She quickly turned her attention to the others again, but a love song filling the room with its familiar words and melody didn't make forgetting any easier.

After helping Gayle clear away the soup bowls and bring in the salad, she sat down and found Matt watching her again. "Penny for your thoughts," she ventured, sounding braver than she felt.

He smiled, but his blue eyes were serious. "Cost you a thousand dollars."

"That's far too expensive for me," she said lightly and began to eat the vinaigrette salad and the mouthwatering boeuf bourguignon. She hoped he wasn't thinking that she was one of those . . . women he picked up and dropped just as quickly.

The conversation drifted to the June wedding. After a few minutes, Paula noticed Matt's overconcentration on buttering his French bread, and she took pity on him. After all, they were both in the same situation—happy for their friends, but feeling left out. "Are you ready for the Yucatan trip?" she asked him.

"Almost. I do have to spend most of next week in Sunnyvale to tie up loose ends."

Gayle raised a hand toward them. "Don't forget the pretrip meeting here tomorrow night. Paula, why don't you tell Matt about Dr. Zayere while Josh and I clear the table."

Paula told Matt the gist of it, enjoying the memories herself. Gayle had become enthused with archeology at the university, and her enthusiasm had been contagious. Her favorite professor, Dr. Zayere, had made ancient peoples come so alive, the two of them had even joined him and others on a New Mexico dig for a week last summer. "It was marvelous," she finished, "the experience of a lifetime—and addicting."

"I've never been on a dig," Matt responded, "but that's exactly how I felt about the ruins in Greece and Italy—addicted."

"And I thought you'd kept your nose to the grindstone these last few years!"

He laughed softly. "I did break away occasionally."

She recalled the travel pieces she would be writing for the *Santa Rosita Times* and told them about it. "Did you suggest my writing the articles to Tom Timmons?" she asked Gayle, who was carrying in a luscious chocolate torte.

Gayle shrugged. "I might have dropped a hint. After all, you did work for them all those summers."

Paula shook her head. "Anyhow, I'm going to do it." She turned to Matt. "I'm supposed to tell you that Tom wouldn't mind your doing the photography. He's upping the pay to ten dollars per published picture."

Gayle and Josh laughed uproariously.

Matt chuckled, then turned serious. "I'll think about it."

"You're joking," Paula said.

"Not at all," he replied.

The evening ended with all four of them in the living room studying a map of Mexico's Yucatan Peninsula and tracing their route. They perused the Yucatan brochures on the coffee table. Besides exotic Mayan pyramids, there were colonial cathedrals, thatch-roofed houses of contemporary Mayans in

37

native costumes, and turquoise Caribbean waters curling onto sandy white beaches.

"I almost forgot," Paula said, handing Gayle her check for the trip. She felt an instant's concern; the amount was a major portion of her savings.

"I almost forgot to tell you," Gayle commented somewhat uneasily, "Vanessa Starke Packard may be coming."

Suddenly numb, Paula turned toward Matt.

"Vanessa?" he asked with an odd expression.

Gayle nodded as if it were the most natural development in the world. "Her mother and stepfather had signed up, but the doctor advised her stepfather not to go. Vanessa just happens to be visiting her parents. It seems she's getting a divorce."

Paula's spirits plummeted. Of all people to have along!

"She called the agency this afternoon about tomorrow night's pretrip meeting."

"More of the old school group," Matt murmured offhandedly.

Paula made an effort at nonchalance. "How many from Santa Rosita High does that make?"

"Fourteen," Gayle replied. "And twelve from the city."

"A nice-sized group," Josh commented.

The discussion drifted to the various people who would travel with them, and Paula tried to focus on that.

Moments later, she was surprised to find Matt slipping an arm around her shoulders. "Ready to go home?" he asked with a twinkle in his eyes.

"Yes . . . of course." The feeling of his fingers through the light wool of her sleeves sent a shiver down her spine.

As they left, Paula kissed Gayle and Josh again. "I'm so happy for both of you. I can't think of anyone I'd rather see in love."

Josh chuckled, and the amusement dancing in Gayle's eyes said, "I can and it's you!"

Paula was pleased that Matt drove straight home. As he stopped in her driveway, she reached to open her own door. "I can let myself out. . . ."

But he was too fast and his hands grasped her shoulders, turning her, gathering her to him as her heart thumped wildly.

Her brain flashed, Resist! Her emotions were reeling, and in the moonlight his ardent gaze overcame all reason.

"Paula," he whispered, just as she had once dreamed he might. He tilted her chin toward his face. His warm lips explored hers tentatively, tasting, searching, testing for resistance.

She tried to push away, but suddenly she was helpless against the rising insistence of his lips. *Oh, Matt!* her heart cried out. Her arms moved around him naturally, her hands caressing his neck. *So this is what it's like to really be kissed,* an inner voice said, and a silvery shower of light exploded behind her eyelids. *Oh, Matt!* her heart cried again and again.

For long moments, she forgot all of her doubts, but finally sanity returned. She fought for control, bringing her hands against his chest to press away. "No!" she whispered. "Please, no."

Though Matt softened his hold on her, he kept her close in his arms. "It's not as if we don't know each other, Paula." Her pulse beat wildly again, and he drew her closer.

"Don't!" she pleaded quickly. "Please let me go in."

He hesitated, then moved away. At her front door he asked, "May I pick you up tomorrow night for the meeting?"

She occupied herself with digging in her handbag for the house key. "Thank you, I'm not sure. . . ."

"Paula?" Matt whispered, and she knew that he wanted to kiss her again.

She quickly unlocked and opened the door. "Thank you!

Thanks for driving!" She tried to slip in, but his hand was on her waist, and he turned her toward him to drop a kiss on her forehead.

"Good night, Paula," he murmured huskily. "I'll pick you up at ten to seven."

She nodded unthinkingly. When she closed the door, she realized how unsteady her knees felt, how foolish she'd been to let this happen. As she made her way slowly upstairs, she recalled that his own mother had called him a playboy. And her mother had warned her. Paula told herself firmly, *Never, ever again!*

On Sunday morning she agonized over whether she should let Matt pick her up for the pretrip meeting, conjuring up excuses to avoid him. She could play sick, but then she'd miss hearing Dr. Zayere; moreover, she didn't want to lie. Perhaps she could ask Gayle about coming early to help with refreshments. That seemed the better choice, although she'd have to call Matt to tell him.

When she telephoned Gayle, her response was, "Wonderful! We'd love to have your help!"

In the afternoon, just moments before she talked herself into calling Matt, he phoned her. "I just saw Gayle at the supermarket," he began. "They need help to move furniture around, and she said that you were giving her a hand with refreshments. We'd better leave around six."

Paula swallowed hard. "Fine." So much for deviousness.

As she dressed in her powder blue skirt and sweater, she wondered why she felt she must avoid Matt. She would never again trust men. . . .

By the time he arrived, she had tired of analyzing herself. She would have a fine time, enjoy Dr. Zayere and her fellow tourists, and walk home if she felt like it. After all, this was no date—it was only a ride to Gayle's house!

40

At the door, Matt met her with a steadfast gleam in his eyes. "Ready, Paula?" He looked terribly respectable in his pale blue cashmere pullover sweater, white shirt open at the collar, and gray wool slacks—very much the innocent gentleman, as if there'd been nothing between them last night.

"Ready," she replied, though not certain for what. She was wearing her navy blue coat to avoid his helping her into it, his being too close.

"Drive or walk?" he asked.

After considering her high heels and the possibility of Matt grabbing her if she stumbled on the sidewalk, she decided, "Drive, I guess."

In the blue Porsche she remembered last night's kiss and stared straight ahead. Matt rambled on about the unseasonably warm weather and then about the Yucatan as if he'd forgotten what had happened between them. Moments later, he announced, "Here we are."

Inside Gayle's house, Paula hurried to the kitchen, and Matt headed for the living room to help Josh. She occupied herself with arranging nuts, cheeses, and crackers in bowls and plates, and with washing the dusty punch glasses.

"All done," Gayle said. "We can take everything into the dining room."

Paula hung back.

Her friend laughed. "What's gotten into you?"

A flush rose on Paula's face. "I guess I was thinking."

Gayle looked at her suspiciously, but said nothing as they walked into the living room. Matt and Josh were taping a map of Mexico to the huge Tudor fireplace. Rows of folding chairs augmented the living room furniture for the meeting.

"Everything looks super!" Gayle exclaimed.

"So do you two," Josh returned.

Matt turned to Paula. "You look very nice in blue."

She allowed herself a fast smile. "Thank you."

"It happens to be my favorite color," he added.

"Who would have guessed?" Josh teased. "Blue car, blue sweater, blue suits . . ."

Matt chuckled, but Paula decided she should have guessed. He probably suspected she'd worn her powder blue sweater and skirt to please him. Between her outfit and his pullover sweater, people would very likely be amused; the two of them resembled over-age high school steadies.

The doorbell rang, and Gayle hurried to answer it.

Paula speculated that it wouldn't be Vanessa Starke Packard arriving early. Vanessa struck her as the type who arrived fashionably late. Evan Walker was out of town. Paula barely knew any of the expected guests, all of whom were older. It seemed that no one else from her and Gayle's high school class could afford the time or the money for the trip.

Gayle ushered in an elderly couple and introduced them.

By seven o'clock the living and dining rooms were crowded with excited fellow travelers sipping punch while discussing what to pack and where to buy the best bargains in the Yucatan.

Dr. Zayere, a cherub of a man with heavy glasses, was one of the last to arrive, and Paula stepped forward to greet him. "How wonderful of you to come to speak to us."

"My pleasure, Paula," he responded with his usual enthusiasm. "It's worth it just to see you and Gayle again, to know that my teaching interested you enough to visit the Yucatan." They chatted a moment longer, then it was time for him to make his way through the crowd among the folding chairs to the front of the room.

Paula sat down in the last row near the door to let in latecomers and found Matt coming to sit beside her.

42

"Are you upset about last night?" he asked.

She lifted her shoulders lightly. "I'd rather not discuss it." Like Tony, he would probably only try to sweet-talk his way into her favor again—until another woman came along.

Matt's arm moved protectively around the back of her folding chair, and she couldn't help remembering last night in his car. "Listen, Paula—"

Gayle clapped her hands for attention at the front of the room, and Paula quickly turned away from Matt as the meeting began, wondering what it was he'd been about to say. When he removed his arm from the back of her chair and faced forward, she was torn between regret and relief.

It wasn't until Dr. Zayere was introduced that Vanessa and her mother made their entrance, capturing every eye in the room. Vanessa, as sleek as ever, wore an exquisite leopard jacket over black slacks and sweater. With her amber eyes and raven hair in a French twist, she was even more beautiful than she'd been as a fashion model during high school.

Paula rose to show her to the empty seats, but Vanessa's eyes swept past her to Matt.

"Well, look who we have here," she murmured silkily.

As if she didn't know he was going on the trip! Paula thought with annoyance, then felt a stab of remorse. Despite her dislike of Vanessa, she'd always felt a little sorry for her too. It couldn't have been easy for Vanessa, being a cocktail waitress's daughter from the wrong side of Santa Rosita, struggling to make money and to be popular too. Finally her mother had married an elderly bar owner associated with organized crime. Then there'd been plenty of money for transforming Vanessa into what they considered high society—an undertaking begun while she was a senior in high school, after Matt was at Stanford.

Matt helped the women remove their coats, and Paula's

eyes went to Vanessa's figure—slim except for her voluptuous bosom, which was conspicuously displayed in a low-cut black sweater. Despite her impending divorce, she seemed no worse for wear; if anything, she was more beautiful. And, of course, wealthier.

Paula dug in her handbag for a small notebook and pencil. Dr. Zayere was already speaking, and she forced herself to concentrate on his words. She would need to learn all that she could for the travel articles.

"The ancient peoples who inhabited the Yucatan Peninsula of Mexico and much of the surrounding land came from the unknown, out of the deeps of mystery," he said with his usual dramatic flair. "We call them the Maya. But they had different names for themselves, many of which are now lost. For an amazing fifteen centuries . . . *fifteen centuries!* . . . they flourished in Middle America. Between A.D. 250 and 900 they shaped a magnificent civilization—a civilization that included splendid palaces and soaring temples."

Dr. Zayere was as ebullient as ever, Paula thought with pleasure and hoped that she could bring such enthusiasm to her articles. She noticed that Matt was taking notes. It wasn't terribly surprising since he'd been a brilliant student and was probably interested in ancient civilizations too.

"They were an amazing people," Dr. Zayere said. "While Europeans still lived in caves, the Maya's astronomy was so precise that their calendar was as accurate as ours today! They plotted the course of celestial bodies so effectively that the priests could predict both lunar and solar eclipses . . . much to the awe of their followers. They calculated the path of the elusive planet, Venus—our morning and evening star."

As Dr. Zayere stepped to the map of Mexico and Central America behind him, Paula glanced at Matt and found him looking at her. Surprised, she smiled uncertainly and turned her attention to the map again.

"This thumblike protrusion jutting out between the Gulf of Mexico and the Caribbean Sea is the Yucatan Peninsula," Dr. Zayere explained. "Only recently have scholars lighted the dim past of the Maya who lived in the Yucatan. The Mayan city-states and dynasties are beginning to come into focus."

He paused dramatically. "What emerges is a peaceful people who practiced esoteric religious rites in the vastness of the jungle until they merged with a warlike people. Later, during the Post-Classic Period—about A.D. 900 until the Spanish conquest—a sixteenth-century Spanish bishop said this about the changing Maya: 'The occupation to which they are most inclined is trading.'"

Matt chuckled. "Sounds like they fell from academic geniuses to businessmen."

Paula smiled. She noticed that Vanessa looked up at him, perplexed, before inspecting her bright, coral fingernails again.

As Dr. Zayere continued, Paula was grateful for the review, jotting the dates of the Mayan civilizations.

"When I consider the remnants of the Mayan civilization," Dr. Zayere said, "it's always with a sense of tragedy. The rise and fall of the Maya bring to light not only man's capacity for greatness, but also his affinity for doom."

Paula reflected on her own affinity for doom with men as she saw Vanessa's hand resting on Matt's arm while she whispered something that brought a smile to his lips.

Dr. Zayere continued. "We have learned about the ancient Mayans in numerous ways: through archeology with its unearthing of buildings, stelae, and inscriptions; through chronicles in which the Mayans presented a version of their own history—one even mentioned a great flood such as we read about in the Bible; and through accounts by Spanish conquerors and friars who recorded Mayan practices. And, finally, we have the remaining Maya."

"There are Maya living today?" someone asked.

"Yes, a few who survived in scattered villages. Some still speak the old languages, but their bloodlines are diluted and their distant past forgotten. Today they are more apt to use a primitive slash-and-burn method of farming; during the peak of their civilization they used sophisticated agricultural techniques that supported a large population."

Vanessa sat up in interest when the talk turned to the elite class, the small group of priests and leaders charged with preserving knowledge.

"These people understood art, architecture, engineering, and astronomy. In return, they led privileged lives. Luxuries like jade, feathers, and jaguar pelts were reserved for them," Dr. Zayere said. "When the elite traveled, it was the duty of the commoners to carry them in litters on their shoulders."

After Dr. Zayere concluded his talk, Vanessa said, "They could have kept the feathers, but I wouldn't have minded the jade and the jaguar coats."

"You're already wearing a leopard skin jacket," Matt pointed out.

Vanessa smiled wryly. "But I could use a jaguar full-length coat."

The meeting ended with Gayle explaining final details of the itinerary and where to meet at the Los Angeles airport. After it was over, Paula quickly slipped into the dining room to refill the punch bowl.

When the crowd began to thin, Paula flinched to see Vanessa and her mother talking with Dr. Zayere, and Matt standing behind them. Passing by, she overheard the women ask the professor about buying pre-Columbian artifacts.

"That's strictly against the law," Dr. Zayere said. "The authorities take a dim view of it."

"But it is done, isn't it?" Vanessa asked.

"Yes, unfortunately it is." He glanced away momentarily, as if he were anxious to escape.

Paula stepped forward. "Thank you again for the excellent talk, Dr. Zayere. It was a marvelous review for me."

"My pleasure, Paula. Now, if we can find Gayle, I should be on my way."

Paula spotted Gayle and waved her over.

As they escorted Dr. Zayere to the door, Paula turned and caught a glimpse of the living room. Matt stood with an arm around Vanessa's shoulder, and she had an arm around his waist. Paula's emotions swung from shock to hurt, then to anger. They were laughing with old school friends, and it struck Paula that they looked just as they had walking home together from high school years ago: the stunningly beautiful Vanessa Starke and the handsome Matt Montgomery.

Paula grabbed her coat from the entry closet. "I'll walk Dr. Zayere to his car," she said to Gayle.

"That's not necessary," he demurred.

Gayle frowned.

"I'm walking home anyway," Paula stated firmly. She slipped into her coat as she stepped outdoors. "Please tell Matt a bit later, Gayle."

"Oh, Paula!" Gayle protested in dismay.

"See you," Paula replied before hurrying down the walk with Dr. Zayere. She did not want to compete with Vanessa or any other woman for a man—particularly not a man like Matt, whose interest in women was fleeting.

After saying good-night to Dr. Zayere, she rushed home in the moonlight. Why invite more heartache, more torment by waiting for Matt? she reflected, already angry with herself for her interest in him. Wouldn't Matt just turn out to be like Tony . . . and most other men?

chapter
3

IN THE AFTERNOONS PAULA SUNNED herself by the neighborhood pool, researching the Yucatan in books she'd picked up
at the library; she was determined to be reasonably knowledgeable about the Mexican peninsula by Saturday. She tried
to forget Matt, yet thoughts of him cropped up continually.

Every time she opened the gate to the pool complex, she
hoped he'd be there, then assiduously avoided "his chaise
lounge." As if that would help matters—she knew he was in
Sunnyvale on business!

At least I'm acquiring a deep tan, she thought, thankful to
an unknown Swedish ancestor from whom she'd inherited her
coloring. Moreover, she was learning a great deal about the
ancient Mayan civilization, the Spanish conquistadors, and
modern Cancun.

On Friday while packing her suitcase, she cast occasional
glances out her upstairs window at the street in front of
Matt's house. No sign of him. He'd probably meet them at
the airport tomorrow, flying directly in from the Bay Area.

She tried to focus on packing her wardrobe for the trip.
Fortunately this time the prospects were more exciting than
when she'd fled Phoenix. If the *Times* articles worked out well,
perhaps she'd do more travel writing; perhaps she could
eventually become a travel editor for a newspaper.

After dinner Gayle phoned. "Josh is driving his family's old station wagon so we can fit in all of the luggage."

"I don't mind sitting in back with a suitcase or two," Paula said. Most of their luggage would fit into a car's trunk; everyone was allowed only a large suitcase and a carry-on case.

"You're sitting in back with Matt," Gayle announced.

"With Matt?"

Gayle ignored her surprise. "And this time you're not walking!"

"Not likely!" Los Angeles was over an hour's drive away. "I thought he'd be meeting us at the airport. You didn't say—"

"He's meeting us at nine tomorrow morning at his house. I didn't tell you for fear you'd flee again."

"Oh, Gayle. I'm not *that* bad!"

"Almost," Gayle responded in a wry tone.

Had Matt arrived home early and purposely stayed out of sight? Perhaps he was furious with her for walking home from the meeting at Gayle's house. Most probably he'd been so preoccupied with Vanessa that he'd forgotten her anyhow.

The next morning, moments after Josh's station wagon pulled into her driveway, Matt came striding up the sidewalk.

Paula glanced at herself in the entry mirror and was amazed at the cheerful young woman whose blue-green eyes sparkled with anticipation. She patted back her hair, then opened the door before he could knock. "Hi," she said, only a trifle unnerved at the sight of him.

"Good morning, Paula," he responded with a dazzling smile.

Sunshine streamed through the trees, dappling her and Matt with its golden warmth. For an instant it reminded her of the morning she had brought him the armful of roses from the garden.

"All ready?" he asked.

50

"Ready!" His wire-rimmed sunglasses hid his eyes, but he didn't sound angry with her for walking out on him. He probably hadn't considered their going to Gayle's house together a date either.

She gathered up her shoulder bag, attaché and blue carry-on case, then found herself smiling at his casual light blue blazer and navy pants. People might suspect they'd planned coordinating outfits again! She'd worn her navy blazer and a light blue skirt.

He lifted her suitcase with ease. "You look like a California girl," he said.

"A California girl? Oh, the tan!" She laughed, pulling the front door shut behind her. "I lounged around the pool afternoons."

Sunlight glimmered around them as they turned to start down the sidewalk. In the distance a bird sang and leaves fluttered on the trees. She found Matt looking at her with a curious smile. "Isn't it a glorious morning?" she asked.

"Yes," he replied. "Yes, it certainly is."

She had the sudden impression she was embarking on the adventure of her lifetime—and that it concerned Matt and the Yucatan and . . . something she couldn't quite put a finger on.

In the car, Gayle and Josh looked as ebullient as she felt.

"Excited?" Gayle asked.

"I can't wait," Paula confessed. She glanced at Matt to see if he thought her childish.

"Anticipation is supposed to be half the fun of a trip," he remarked with genuine enthusiasm.

"You'd think we were a carful of kids starting out for a circus," Josh said as they pulled out of the driveway and started down the tree-lined street.

"Aren't we?" Gayle inquired brightly, and they all laughed.

Saturday morning traffic was still light in Santa Rosita; even the freeways were surprisingly uncrowded as they

51

approached the Los Angeles airport area. Josh parked the car in a lot, and within minutes, they were sitting on an airport bus, then unloading bags beside the airport terminal.

As they checked their luggage Josh said to Paula and Matt, "No sense in you two sitting around with Gayle and me. We'll have to sit at the gate to gather the group. Why don't you have a cup of coffee?"

"How about it?" Matt asked Paula.

"Fine." She'd been too excited to have breakfast, and coffee sounded good. Besides, he'd removed his sunglasses, and his blue eyes were terribly convincing.

"I'll take your carry-on case," Gayle offered.

"If you're sure—" Paula gratefully handed over her case, and Josh took Matt's camera bag.

"Are you really going to take pictures for the *Santa Rosita Times?*" she teased Matt as they made their way through the crowded airport.

"Why not?" he replied with an unabashed smile. "I've always enjoyed photography. Besides, you're not the only one who's unemployed."

"Unemployed?" She laughed. From what Gayle had implied, Matt could retire for life.

Heading for the cafeteria, she realized this was the first time they had been alone since they'd driven to Dr. Zayere's talk. She owed Matt an apology for walking out on him. Finally she managed, "I'm sorry about leaving so abruptly from Gayle's house Sunday night. It's just that I . . ."

"Let's forget it," he said, looking away over the airport crowd.

For an instant she suspected that he'd been hurt, but how could that be? After all, *he* had kissed her passionately one night, then put his arm around Vanessa the next. Still, it might have been merely a companionable gesture on his part, a response to Vanessa's arm around him.

In the cafeteria Paula bypassed the crowd and headed for the coffee. Matt stopped at the pie counter. "I'll get seats," she called over to him, and he nodded. Paying for her coffee, she spied two seats being vacated in the dimly lit room.

Hurrying to them, she sat down and placed her attaché case on the adjacent chair. As she settled back, she watched Matt in the cashier's line. Women of all ages stared at him, reminding her that it would be especially foolish to become involved with him. If only she'd evaded his kiss!

After paying, he stood in front of the cashier with his orange plastic tray looking for her.

Paula rose. "Over here!"

He approached grinning. "I was waylaid by the pies."

She laughed. "And two pieces! Do you always eat pie for breakfast?"

"Only with conspirators," he answered, placing a wedge of pie in front of her. "I hope you like blueberry."

"I love it, thank you. How did you know?"

He disposed of the cafeteria tray and grinned. "We both apparently like blue."

"You noticed." She was astonished to find herself blushing and quickly turned to her pie. Trying a forkful, she thought it surprisingly delicious for cafeteria fare.

"I've noticed a good deal about you lately," Matt said.

"That I've grown up?" she ventured.

A mischievous glow lit his eyes. "Yes, that you've certainly grown up."

"Anything else?"

"That you look . . . ," he began, but his airy response faltered for an instant. "Twice as delicious as blueberry pie."

She darted an incredulous look at him. "Really!"

He chuckled.

She turned away from his disconcerting eyes and concentrated on eating the pie. What sort of a line does he use on

53

Vanessa? she thought. Surely nothing that corny. He'd do better with jade and jaguar coats with her!

Later, in the boarding lounge, most of the Santa Rosita group had already gathered, although Vanessa and her mother were nowhere in sight.

"Paula! Paula Ingraham!"

She turned to find Evan Walker hurrying toward her. "Evan! It's good to see you again."

"It's been a few years," he said, shaking her hand. His soft brown eyes brimmed with pleasure from behind fashionable horn-rimmed glasses. "You look wonderful . . . just wonderful!"

She laughed. "Thanks." If Evan said so, she must look fine. "You look great yourself," she added, watching his flush of delight. He'd matured, but it didn't distract from his boyish handsomeness. She supposed he was twenty-five now since he'd been two years ahead of her in school. His shoulders had broadened as if he worked out in a gym. Just under six feet, he looked attractive with his dark brown, stylishly cut hair.

The loudspeaker crackled. "Now boarding Flight 329—"

"See you later, Paula," he said. "I have to get my things. I'm glad you're on the trip."

She smiled, pleased Evan was going too.

Half of the group had boarded the plane when Vanessa and her mother arrived—Vanessa looking like a movie star in a white silk pants suit, her gleaming black hair again up in an elegant French twist. Heads turned all over the boarding lounge to admire her, but she proceeded directly to Matt.

"I had a ship-to-shore call at the last minute," she explained breathlessly. "Seems I'm staying on after this tour with friends in Cozumel. They're sailing their yacht over from the Mediterranean now."

Matt raised his eyebrows. "Must be a good-sized yacht."

"They're Arabs in oil," she answered blithely. "You're welcome to join us."

He looked impressed. "Thank you. I'd like to think about it, if I may."

He certainly would think about that! Paula thought, disheartened. Stepping into the boarding tunnel ahead of them, she recalled reading about Cozumel, a Mexican island on the Caribbean. It sounded exactly like Vanessa's kind of place—where the jet set had fun in the sun.

On the DC-9, Paula made her way to her window seat, struggling to avoid disappointment. She stowed her blue carry-on case under the seat and forced a bright smile when Matt arrived to sit beside her. He would probably be sitting with Vanessa if she hadn't been so late. Glancing back, she saw that Vanessa and her mother were settling several rows behind them on the other side of the aisle.

When the plane roared across the runway, Paula pulled out a paperback about the nineteenth-century discovery of the Mayan civilization. Before she could begin to read, Matt was full of questions about the book, then about her research.

"I've always been fascinated by ancient civilizations," he remarked. "I envy you and Gayle taking part in an archeological dig. I'd like to try it myself."

"It was wonderful." She eyed him thoughtfully. "I'd think that archeology would be the last thing to interest a businessman. After all, no one makes money digging up the past . . . except those who loot ruins and sell artifacts."

He chuckled. "There are businessmen and there are businessmen. I've yet to loot anything, let alone sell artifacts. I'm still pretty much the Matt Montgomery who grew up next door to you."

"Oh?" she replied. "I rather doubt that."

He gave a laugh. "Well, maybe not quite."

When the Fasten Seat Belts sign winked off, Gayle and Josh made their way down the aisle, stopping to say a few words to all of the tour members.

Paula glanced in their direction. "Aren't they a beautiful couple?"

"They do look good together," he agreed, amused. "Josh looks as happy as a—" He stopped, his color deepening.

"As happy as what?" she laughed, certain he'd nearly said "happy as a fool."

"As happy as I've ever seen him," Matt answered, embarrassed.

As their conversation continued, she recalled that Gayle and Josh had always known each other, but Josh was seven years older than Gayle—just like Matt and herself. "Do you know how they happened to get together?" she asked.

"Josh said they met at a church dinner. His parents had invited him to hear a speaker about the space program, and Gayle was serving desserts." Matt grinned. "Josh always did have a sweet tooth."

Paula smiled. "And Gayle's always helping at church. I don't think she's missed a Sunday in years since her father's death, and that was back in grade school."

"So that's why . . . ," Matt began. He hesitated, then apparently changed his line of thought. "Josh attends church now too. I can't get over how he's changed."

"Oh, really?"

"He was turning into quite a drinker. He was pretty unnerved, being expected to follow in the family footsteps. They're a formidable force in the community."

She nodded. "He did seem shy."

"Law school changed him a little," Matt said, "but he was still basically insecure. At first I thought his falling in love with Gayle made him turn around, but it's more than that. He's given over his life to Christ." The tone of Matt's voice seemed carefully neutral, as if disguising his impression that Josh had gone off the deep end.

Paula blinked. "Really?"

"I take it you don't attend church anymore?" he said.

"I make it for Christmas and weddings."

She'd gone to Sunday school with Gayle when they were girls but had stopped in her teens. She recalled singing with the children's choir on a Youth Sunday when Matt had spoken from the pulpit, though she couldn't remember what they had sung, nor what he had said. She'd been in fourth grade then; he, a junior in high school. She supposed he had drifted away from church too.

Matt extracted the airline magazine from the seat pocket in front of him and opened it, bringing the discussion to an end.

Paula looked out the plane window. Los Angeles and its endless suburbs and smog lay behind them. Craggy foothills rose above the mist in the valleys, and here and there the sun shimmered on lakes and rivers, transforming them into golden mirrors. An appropriate perspective from which to think about God, though she rarely did. It was an uncomfortable subject, and she wished it hadn't been broached between them.

The airline's lunch featured a beef tostada. And, of course, there was "Coca," as the Mexican flight attendant called the cola given to everyone. "The national drink of Mexico," she joked with Paula and Matt.

After lunch Vanessa stopped by in the aisle. "Just getting my exercise." Her amber eyes took in the two of them, but she did not return Paula's smile. She handed Matt a brochure. "It tells about Cozumel. Just in case you decide to go."

"Thanks," he replied.

"Several airlines fly there from Cancun all day long."

"You've been there before?" he asked her.

"Yes, but I've always flown in from Mexico City or Paris."

Matt glanced from her to the brochure. "Very interesting."

"Keep it for a while," Vanessa responded. She leaned over to whisper in his ear, the V of her silk jacket affording him a glimpse of her ample cleavage.

Paula looked away.

When Vanessa moved on down the aisle, Paula glanced at the map of Cozumel in the brochure Matt was perusing; she especially noted an *isla de la pasion*. She didn't remember much high school Spanish, but she knew an "island of passion" when she saw it. Turning to the window, she reminded herself that what went on between Matt and Vanessa was none of her affair. She looked out at the majestic mountain ranges protruding from the earth.

After a while Matt asked, "What's out there now?" Unfastening his seat belt, he leaned across her to glance out.

The faint muskiness of his aftershave affected her oddly again. "A wrinkled land," she replied, remembering the phrase from her research. "When the King of Spain asked Cortez what Mexico looked like, he crumpled a piece of paper in his hand to show how mountainous it was."

"Is that so?" he asked with a peculiar smile, his face close to hers.

She nodded and was relieved when he sat back in his seat. Just sitting next to him was more than enough for her to handle, she thought, entranced with his broad hand on the armrest. As he refastened his seat belt, she averted her eyes, hoping that he didn't sense her interest.

"I take it the Yucatan won't be mountainous," he said.

"It's flat from what I've read. But it's so isolated from mainland Mexico by mountains that the Yucatecs once planned to form their own nation. The children were educated in New Orleans or Europe, and their second—and sometimes first—language was French."

"You're a fount of information," he said, grinning.

She shrugged and opened her book. He probably found her a fount of dullness compared to Vanessa.

When they deplaned in Monterrey for Mexican Immigration, Paula purposely hung back so that Matt wouldn't feel obligated to be with her. But he waited, too, until Gayle and Josh joined them, and they walked to the modern airport building together.

Inside, she had only to present a copy of her birth certificate and her tourist card. She noted that Matt, like Vanessa and many of the others, had a passport. Either identification was acceptable with a tourist card, but she felt unsophisticated by comparison. She'd made short trips to Mexico from California, but never to a country requiring a passport. Matt and Vanessa obviously had.

When they reboarded the plane, she was grateful that Matt sat with her again.

Two hours later, they landed in the darkness for a ten-minute stop at Cancun. Most of the passengers deplaned, and only a few tourists and Mexicans boarded for the final leg of the trip to Merida.

"Almost there," Matt said, pulling out his itinerary and sharing it with her as the plane took off again.

Their tour would begin in sixteenth-century Merida, where they'd visit the Mayan ruins of Uxmal and Kabah. Then they'd be bused to the famous ruin of Chichen Itza and stay in a nearby Mayan village. Last came the modern island resort of Cancun for a rest on the beaches and for visiting the ancient Mayan's coastal ruin of Tulum and other nearby points of interest.

Despite her exhaustion, Paula's anticipation mounted. Finally the plane swooped down into the darkness, heading for Merida's lighted runway. "We're here!" She might have applauded if it weren't so unsophisticated.

In the sparkling new airport building, porters dealt with their luggage while the Santa Rosita group met their darkly handsome Mexican tour guide, Jacob. Immaculate in his tan safari-type suit, he smilingly gathered everyone together and led them out into the jasmine-scented night air.

"Our bus," he announced, directing them to the first of three buses waiting along the curb. The small airport parking lot was nearly empty; there was no sound of planes or cars anywhere.

"It's not quite like L.A.'s airport," Paula observed.

"Thank goodness," Matt responded.

She was surprised to find him at her side since Vanessa seemed determined to be near him. Her mother, Mrs. Perotta, walked more slowly, belying her youthful appearance and thwarting Vanessa's efforts to catch up with Matt.

It seemed only a few minutes before their luggage was loaded and their bus headed through the dark countryside. "Merida is a city of four hundred thousand people," Jacob said into the microphone by the front seat. "We have the lowest crime rate in all of Mexico. Still, you must be careful on the streets. It is not quite heaven."

Matt casually slid his arm around the back of Paula's seat. She felt happily enfolded by his nearness, though she didn't know whether he was displaying affection or only needed to change position. If he were as stiff as she was from sitting all day, it was most likely the latter. In any case, she had to make mental notes for the travel articles and write her impressions before she went to bed.

Jacob continued with details of the area, then of their itinerary. When they entered the city, he pointed out the sights. "Merida is called the 'white city' for its cleanliness, its buildings, and the people's white clothing."

The city did look exceptionally clean, and the Spanish colonial buildings appeared more European than the red tile-roofed buildings of other Mexican cities she'd seen. The lighted parks were lovely, but nearly deserted since it was after ten o'clock. Driving into the downtown area, Jacob added, "And here we have the *zocalo*, Merida's main plaza, with its sixteenth-century cathedral."

Paula gazed out her window. Great Indian laurel trees sprawled over the vast expanse of walks, benches, and bandstand area. Around the plaza, the magnificent cathedral and Spanish colonial buildings were flooded with light, in breathtaking contrast to the midnight-blue sky with its luminous clouds.

"Across the street you can ride in our *calesas,* the antique horse-drawn cabs," Jacob said.

From the bus window, Paula and Matt looked out at the high-wheeled carriages, each with a horse and a driver waiting for passengers. As the bus stopped for a traffic light, a young couple engaged one of the calesas, and climbed into the seats. The young man dropped the rolled shades over the open side and back windows, but there was nothing across the front to prevent watching him passionately claim the young woman in his arms.

Everyone chuckled, and Paula cast a glance at Matt.

He grinned, but said nothing.

She supposed he had kissed dozens of women. Just on this bus with its twenty-six passengers, he had kissed her . . . and certainly Vanessa.

"Around the corner is your hotel, one of Merida's finest," Jacob announced, then gave them final instructions for meeting in the morning for their tour of the city.

As she climbed out of the bus into the silky night air, she glimpsed a great white colonial hotel. Her exhaustion faded, replaced by a surge of exhilaration. Just ahead on the street was a group of *mariachis* in their elegant black and silver costumes and sombreros, carrying their guitars and other instruments. Delighted, she crossed the street with her group to the hotel.

Inside the hotel's vast white entry and reception salon, roughly hewn beams latticed the soaring ceiling, European carved doors opened to a garden restaurant aptly named Le

61

Jardin, and white marble floors led everywhere. She followed the others toward the dark wooden expanse of registration area where white-suited clerks and bell boys waited attentively.

"Isn't it gorgeous?" she began, turning to Matt.

But he had fallen behind her, and Vanessa was just approaching him, reaching out, then resting her hand on his arm.

"Aren't you going to invite me for a ride around the park in a calesa?" she asked with a meaningful smile.

He looked momentarily flustered but Paula heard him say, "Why not?"

"Then what's keeping us?" Vanessa asked smoothly. "Josh can register you, and my mother can register me."

As Matt stepped away with her, Paula saw him glance in her direction. She turned away, her heart plummeting as she stepped to the shortest registration line.

There was no earthly reason why he shouldn't take someone else for a ride around the park. All he had done was to kiss her as if he loved her! He'd said nothing to indicate that they had a special relationship. He had promised nothing, nothing at all.

chapter
4

ROMANTIC MUSIC DRIFTED THROUGH the hotel's courtyard as Paula and Gayle sat at an elegantly appointed breakfast table. Would Matt be down for breakfast? Paula wondered uneasily. And, if so, what could she possibly say to him after last night? If only she could forget his calesa ride with Vanessa.

The huge rubber tree growing in the middle of the garden dining room reminded her to take notes. "I'll have to find out if the trees in the plaza are really Indian laurels." She jotted in her notebook and, turning the page, said, "You know, my research calls those horse-drawn carriages both *calesas* and *calandrias*. Which is correct?"

"Beats me," Gayle said. "You'd better check with Jacob."

Paula drew a huge question mark beside the words. Just the thought of antique carriages and of Matt and Vanessa clippity-clopping off into the night made her spirits droop.

When she looked up, Gayle's green eyes were studying her. "You're still crazy about Matt, aren't you?"

Paula looked down at her notebook. "I don't know. . . ."

"You and your 'I don't knows!' " Gayle replied with a shake of her head. "Someone like Vanessa will walk off with him while you make up your mind. And I've got an idea she's after him again."

"What do you suggest?" She was torn between competing furiously for him and not being vulnerable again. Her only effort this morning, if it could even be called that, was to wear her pale yellow linen sheath with a matching cashmere sweater. It was probably too nice for touring, but she hoped Matt would like it.

"Maybe you should do something to encourage him," Gayle suggested. "Does he have any idea that you care about him?"

Paula recalled their kiss in Matt's car after Gayle's dinner party. If he didn't realize that she was attracted to him after that, how would he ever guess? Or was he, like Tony, so accustomed to kissing women that it meant nothing?

"You're blushing," Gayle said. "I just hope you didn't actually say that you love him."

"It was nothing so rash as that . . . or roller skating past his house. This time, he took all of the initia—" Her voice cracked and tears sprang to her eyes.

Gayle looked heartsick. "I'm sorry. I shouldn't have pried."

"Oh, Gayle, I promised myself this would never happen to me again!" Aware of the busboy approaching behind her, she blinked away the tears and watched him pour steaming dark coffee. When he stepped over to serve Gayle, she turned away from the compassion in her friend's green eyes.

After he left, Gayle said, "You're going to have to fight for Matt."

"But why should I? Did you have to fight for Josh?"

Gayle shook her head. "No, but I would have if I had to."

"You?"

"There are lots of ways to do battle."

"At the moment, I'm not sure Matt or any other man is worth a battle," Paula returned, feeling fractious. "Why should I have to contend for him? Why shouldn't he fight for me?"

"I'm not sure whether I prefer you sad or mad," Gayle said with a conciliatory laugh.

Seconds later, when Matt and Josh walked into the courtyard dining room, Paula struggled with her doubts. Why did he always look as if he'd been created precisely for her?

While Josh planted a kiss on Gayle's forehead, Matt smiled at Paula. "Good morning, sunshine," he said with an appreciative glance at her yellow dress. "You look beautiful here in the garden."

"You too," she replied. If he were going to act as if his moonlit ride should mean nothing to her, she would pretend that it didn't.

"Me, beautiful?" He chuckled and sat down beside her. "You must not have slept well!"

She hadn't slept well at all, agonizing over him and Vanessa, but she certainly was not going to admit that.

Moments later, their waiter presented the menus, and Paula was relieved to turn her attention toward ordering breakfast.

After they had ordered, Matt glanced at her spiral notebook. "I'm all set to play photographer for your articles."

"You're not serious," Paula replied, unconvinced.

"But I am," Matt protested. "I've always hoped that I could travel after selling the company, but I know I'll have to do something besides bask in the sun. I'd like to try more photography."

"You're a workaholic," Josh interjected.

Matt nodded. "Maybe. At any rate, I've been thinking about putting together a photography book—one of those coffee table tomes that rarely makes a photographer any money. I'd slant it for the various businesses of the world—banks, retailers, builders. It would be pictures of their counterparts around the world throughout history."

Josh shot a penetrating look at his friend. "Sounds like a tax write-off."

"I hadn't intended it that way at all," Matt objected. "It's a unique way of looking at the world, being the eye behind a camera. You see life from a different perspective."

"I'll be darned!" Josh exclaimed mildly. "And I felt I knew so much about you."

"There's a lot that you don't know," Matt replied mysteriously.

And what was that supposed to mean? Paula wondered. She turned to watch the waiter serve their fruit plates with slices of orange, papaya, melon, and pineapple.

Over breakfast she and Matt discussed how they might capture the kind of people-oriented photos Tom Timmons had suggested for the *Times* series.

"What's the basic article slant?" Matt inquired. "That's the first question Tom always demanded I ask."

Paula thumbed reluctantly through the pages in her notebook. She would have to show him her tentative opening. What if he considered it inept or entirely stupid? Finally she found it. "Here's the lead. According to the tip sheet, it's supposed to be simple, but all-encompassing, and it's supposed to establish a mood."

She scanned it nervously as he read.

Ancient ruins of the Mayan civilization . . . sixteenth-century Merida . . . thatch-roofed villages of the contemporary Maya . . . ultra-modern Cancun with its turquoise sea and white sandy beaches . . .

Mexico's Yucatan Peninsula, the thumblike protrusion that juts between the Gulf of Mexico and the Caribbean Sea, is a place of amazing contrasts wrought through the ages. It is nearly impossible not to be intrigued by all of them, whether ancient, colonial, primitive or computer-aged.

While he reread it, she picked at her *huevos con chorizo*— scrambled eggs with tomato *salsa* and bits of spicy sausage piled on a corn tortilla.

"A good opening," he said, looking impressed. "I know they're the hardest part of articles."

"Thanks," she responded with relief. "They certainly are for me."

He placed the notebook on the table between them and lifted his coffee cup in a toast. "We're a team!"

"A team," Paula responded with a smile, touching her cup against his. If their relationship amounted to nothing else, at least they would be a working team for the next two weeks.

"How on earth could you use photography from a trip like this for a business project?" Josh asked Matt.

"Simple. Look at this dining room, for instance. It's not just the tree in the middle and the plants that make it unique, it's the Mayan maître d', the Mayan waiters and busboys. They're not only distinctively handsome with those hawk noses, but there's a great dignity about them, an innate courtesy," Matt explained. "Anyone in the hotel business would enjoy pictures capturing those vanishing qualities, merely as a matter of interest if nothing else."

"But which businesses, if any, would want to see Mayan ruins?" Paula asked.

"Architects . . . developers . . . real estate people. Not only the design of the structures, but how such great pyramids were built without the use of the wheel. And they'd want to know how the ancient Mayans coexisted in their cities."

"I see." Paula mulled over other possibilities. "I suppose that even Beverly Hills shop owners might be intrigued or at least amused to see how the contemporary Mayans sell their wares at outdoor markets."

Matt nodded. "Exactly. Maybe I could do a whole series of

books for different professions. The more I think about it, the more I see that a project like this would involve a good bit of writing. I suppose I'm going to need a collaborator."

"You're full of surprises," Gayle said to Matt. She smiled across the table at Paula as if to impress her with what a great team they'd make.

Paula sipped the strong Mexican coffee, considering the possibilities. If Matt really were financially set for life, he could travel all over the world taking pictures for photography books. And, given his business acumen, he'd probably make money on them too. It sounded like a wonderful idea. How she'd love to be a part of it.

Her eyes wandered absently around the dining room, then stopped. At a table just beyond a group of potted palms, Vanessa was watching them intently.

Minutes before nine o'clock Paula stepped out into the morning sunshine in front of the hotel. All around the marble entry, vendors in neat white shirts sold straw hats, white blouses with colorfully embroidered flowers, conch shell and coral jewelry, sisal hemp hammocks, and other wares.

"Straw hat, señorita?" one of the vendors inquired.

"Not now, gracias. Maybe tomorrow when we visit the ruins."

She looked over the busy street scene for her first travel article, which would include Merida and the nearby Mayan ruins. Matt was already taking pictures of vendors and their wares by the hotel across the narrow street.

Above, the sky was a cerulean blue, entirely smogless, despite the cars hurtling by. In the distance the cathedral bell tolled, and she recalled the line by John Donne: Never send to know for whom the bell tolls; it tolls for thee. There was a holiness to the tolling that lent wonder to the magnificent

Sunday morning. She recalled an old saying about the tolling of church bells being echoes of God's voice.

"Over here!" Gayle called out, and Paula hurried to join the Santa Rosita group being herded onto a tour bus.

"Buenos dias," Jacob, their guide, said as he helped her into the bus.

"Buenos dias!" From the front of the bus, she saw that Evan Walker was seated with his group of friends; five had come from the computer company where he worked.

"Ready for some excitement?" Evan asked as she made her way down the aisle.

"I'm ready!" she replied enthusiastically. She was uncertain about saving a seat for Matt; Gayle and Josh took seats across the aisle. When Matt climbed on the bus, he paused to look about; spotting them, he headed for the seat beside her. Was it because she was with Josh and Gayle? Paula wondered. She looked for Vanessa and her mother, then saw them coming out of the hotel. Vanessa wore a black-and-white harlequin print pants ensemble that looked straight out of *Vogue,* and her mother was equally fashionable in an orange silk pants ensemble.

On the bus Vanessa removed her huge dark glasses and slid them atop her upswept black hair with practiced elegance. She appeared annoyed that the only seats remaining were in the back, but produced a smile as she passed Matt. "Good morning," she murmured, her eyes dancing with amusement.

"Good morning, Vanessa," he answered in an even tone. His smile seemed friendly, nothing else.

Mrs. Perotta trailed behind, her upswept black hair an exact copy of Vanessa's. Mother and daughter looked uncannily alike except that the older woman's neck was so wrinkled in contrast to her unlined face that it was apparent she'd had a facelift. Still, she was a striking beauty and had probably attracted many a man during her cocktail waitress days.

"Mrs. Perotta," Matt said with a polite nod.

"Good morning, Matt," she replied coolly as she swept past.

What had taken place between Vanessa and Matt on that calesa ride last night? Paula wondered once again.

The bus door flapped shut and Jacob manned the microphone with the air of a seasoned guide. "Today we will tour Merida," he said as the bus took off. "We begin at the Museum of Anthropology. There you will learn something of the Yucatan and the Mayan people."

Pencil and notebook in hand, Paula watched out the window, noting the narrow one-way streets. Steeples and spires rose over the many parks, and worshipers converged on the churches for the Sunday services.

Within minutes the bus was parked on the elegant Paseo de Montejo, a broad tree-lined avenue. "Here we have the grand mansions of Merida from the days when the city had more millionaires per capita than anywhere else in recent history. In the 1920s and 1930s, this was the sisal hemp capital of the world, and, before that, fortunes were made by exporting dyewood and chicle. If you will step out . . ."

The ornate white Italian Renaissance mansion converted into a museum was surrounded by an elaborate black iron fence wrought by Italian artisans. White Carrara marble lined the front steps.

"Looks like an Italian palazzo," Matt said, snapping picture after picture. "I certainly didn't expect this here."

Behind them, Vanessa and her mother agreed. Mrs. Perotta added rather loudly, "We made a grand tour of Europe the summer Vanessa graduated from high school, you know."

The year Sal Starke had married Joe Perotta—bar owner, bookie, and associate of major crime figures, Paula recalled. Everyone at school had discussed Vanessa's transformation from a cocktail waitress's daughter to a young woman bound for Europe and then for an exclusive Eastern college.

Inside the beautiful museum, spacious rooms with marble floors and crystal chandeliers housed Mayan artifacts from archeological sites. Paula took notes from the maps and charts explaining the region's geography and history.

There were Mayan pots, hatchets, ceramic vases, jewelry, masks, and other artifacts as well as a stone monolith of Chac-Mool, who received human heart sacrifices from live victims for the gods. Among the displays were skulls with drops of jade inlaid in their teeth as well as the wooden apparatus used to flatten heads to prepare them for the gods.

"Deformities such as crossed eyes were revered, and self-mutilation was common," Jacob explained. "Deformed people often became priests. In fact, some Mayans still have good teeth removed and inlaid with gold or jade."

"Ouch," Paula whispered, and Matt agreed as they made their way through the spacious rooms. Suddenly she realized gratefully that her mind had strayed from Tony for quite some time!

"Why all the note-taking, Paula?" Evan Walker asked as they paused by a display of Mayan jewelry.

"We're doing . . . that is, I'm writing some travel articles for the *Santa Rosita Times.*"

"Are you?" He looked impressed, then added upon reflection, "You're just the one to make it interesting. You and Gayle have always been so adventurous and . . . enthusiastic."

"Well, thanks," Paula said, noticing Matt taking in the conversation as they moved along.

"I'll look forward to reading the articles," Evan said.

"*If* I can bring them off," Paula replied. "But you were editor of the school paper. You don't suppose I can get you to proofread them?"

71

He nodded. "My pleasure."

She was thankful that Evan looked better than might have been expected so soon after a divorce.

Later, outside the museum, the Santa Rosita group strolled through the warm morning sunshine to their tour bus. The driver had parked it in the shade of towering trees and, inside, the bus was pleasantly cool.

They drove along slowly on Paseo de Montejo, admiring the many white and pastel mansions dating from the turn of the century. Vanessa and her mother, who'd usurped the seat behind them, kept up a running commentary on how the mansions reminded them of chateaus and villas in France and Italy.

Paula scribbled notes as they rode along. The bus stopped occasionally at spectacular estates so that Matt and others could dash out to take pictures. Palms, laurels, and tamarinds surrounded the lavish houses, and some had avocado, papaya, and mango trees as well. Many of the magnificent mansions were unfortunately covered with moss, mold, and mildew from the tropical climate. According to Jacob, high taxation, the decline of sisal hemp exports, and the lack of willing servants were bringing the owners as well as their houses to ruin.

At the end of Paseo de Montejo the bus stopped beside a new monument to Mexico, an astounding pink stone structure in which the history of the country was carved. Jacob, a transplant from Mexico City, dubbed its style "convoluted Mayan, furious Toltec, and subway modern."

When Matt climbed out with others to take pictures, Vanessa leaned over the seat toward Paula. "Whatever are you taking so many notes for?" she asked.

"Matt and I are doing some articles for the *Santa Rosita Times*," Paula replied.

"Oh, really? And how did you work that?"

"We were asked."

"I see," Vanessa said, sitting back again.

"I'd like to approve any pictures you publish of me," Mrs. Perotta said.

"It's for the travel page," Paula explained. "Tom Timmons doesn't want pictures of us."

"Oh. Well, it will be interesting to read."

The article had better be accurate, Paula thought. Everyone would certainly let Tom Timmons know if she made any errors.

Later they stopped at a clothing factory where the Yucatec national costumes were sold. For women, there were *huipils*— white cotton shifts with short sleeves and bands of colorful embroidery around necklines, sleeves, and hems—to be worn over longer garments with lace hems; for men, white *guayaberas*—loose fitting, pleated shirts.

"Did you find something to buy?" Matt asked her when they met again in the line waiting for their purchases.

His eyes were so disconcerting that it took her a moment before she held up a white cotton blouse with red and green embroidered flowers and parrots. "I didn't think I'd have use for a huipil," she said, although the darkly beautiful sales-women looked lovely in them. "How about you?"

He displayed two bright white guayaberas. "One for my father, one for me." He chuckled. "I don't know if he'll wear his."

"Maybe I should buy one for my father too. But there's no time now."

"We can shop this afternoon," he suggested.

Did that mean he wanted to spend their free afternoon with her? Or did he just think that they should stay together to coordinate the article and photos?

73

Vanessa and Mrs. Perotta joined the line of tourists buying clothing and macrame purses, their arms full of hand-embroidered caftans. "I find them perfect for entertaining," Mrs. Perotta commented.

When everyone boarded the bus again, they drove through the less elegant streets of Merida. Even the modest houses were interesting with their balconies for serenades, and Matt snapped photos at every stop. Occasionally there were thatch-roofed houses among the other buildings, and pink and red hibiscus bloomed everywhere. Here and there windmills turned in the breeze over the rooflines, reminders of when Merida was called "the city of windmills."

As the bus approached their hotel and the Plaza de la Independencia, Jacob explained the need for a city gate in the mid-1500s. "Our Spanish conquerors were not popular," he said. "All of the churches built by them had catacombs leading to the cathedral, which was built like a fortress for safety. They were, after all, surrounded by Mayans."

"A sad situation for everyone," Matt said.

Paula cast a curious look at him, and his deep blue eyes held hers for an instant. Unnerved, she glanced away. She suspected that his thoughts hadn't been on the Spaniards' being surrounded by Mayans.

When they disembarked from the bus in front of their hotel, Josh said, "Why don't the two of you join us for lunch? Jacob recommended a restaurant just off the *zocalo*."

"Are we invited?" Vanessa asked, joining them with her mother. Evan Walker was just behind them too.

"Of course," Josh replied. "The more, the merrier."

Gayle and Josh led the way toward the plaza, and Paula found both Matt and Evan falling into step with her on the crowded sidewalk. Vanessa and her mother trailed behind them.

Wandering past the seventeenth-century university, they glimpsed an inner patio shaped by tiers of Moorish arches. Farther down the block, they browsed in shops where colorful clothing and other tourist wares hung out over the sidewalk.

"We need some pictures across the street," Matt said, nodding toward a lovely old stone church.

Paula thumbed through her guidebook and found a picture of it. "Church of Jesus," she read. "Built in the 1600s."

Nearby in the parklike setting was a graceful marble sculpture of a young mother lightly embracing a child; together, they gazed lovingly at the baby on the mother's lap. The sculptor had captured their tender love so wondrously that the sunshine streaming through the trees seemed to radiate instead from the family. *"Maternidad,"* Paula read. "Motherhood."

"A much over-rated state," Vanessa's mother said archly.

Vanessa made no comment, but Gayle said, "Not to me."

"Nor to me," Paula added, then saw both Matt and Evan glance at her. She supposed she should have kept her mouth shut. Evan's marriage had been disastrous, and a man like Matt, who hadn't married by the age of thirty and who wanted to travel the world to create photography books, would not care to be tied down with a family.

She trailed behind Gayle to a side door of the old stone church. Near the door she heard guitar music—a song of praise so sweet that it touched her heart. She stepped into the cool dark church with Gayle, and the music wafted through the arched sanctuary. Sunlight streamed through stained-glass windows, the colors diffusing on the arches and soaring pillars. After a while, the congregation rose and sang in Spanish.

Paula understood occasional phrases: Bless the Lord, O my

soul. . . . Lord my God, thou art great. . . . Thou art clothed with honor and majesty. . . . What was there about faith that she never quite understood?

When they stepped back out into the sunshine, Matt was snapping pictures of a darkly beautiful girl in her white embroidered huipil; she carried a bag of groceries in each hand and balanced a round tray of onions on her head. Behind her, a plump mother, also garbed in her huipil, carried plastic buckets of groceries in each hand and a huge basket of fresh fruit on her head.

The Plaza de la Independencia was beginning to look familiar after they had seen it on the bus in the morning as well as last night when its Spanish colonial buildings had been flooded with light against the dark sky.

Paula looked up at the great twin-spired cathedral. "The guidebook claims it's the oldest cathedral in Mexico. According to local legend, the cathedral should originally have been built in Lima. The plans for a small cathedral for Merida were supposedly mixed up with Lima's en route from Spain, leaving Merida with the larger church."

"I expect there are lots of interesting stories about churches' beginnings," Matt said. "That might make another good book."

Vanessa raised an eyebrow. "You'd be bored to death with that in no time."

"Maybe so," Matt replied amiably.

Paula hoped he was only being agreeable. She couldn't imagine him a member of the jet set.

Later, as they stepped into the cathedral, she was arrested by not only its size but the stark appearance of the altars.

Vanessa remarked, "I suppose it was sacked like the rest of the churches during the revolution. And, this being Mexico and the land of mañana, they've never restored the vanished furbelows."

76

"But look at that," Paula said, impressed by the large panoramic painting on the wall. According to her guidebook, it depicted a formal call paid on the Spanish conquistador Montejo by the Mayan king of Mani soon after the founding of Merida. At Matt's request she read, "Two months after this call, Tutul Xiu—the most powerful chieftain of the Maya—was converted and baptized Melchor. And he was instrumental in keeping uprisings to a minimum."

"A traitor," Evan remarked.

"It sounds as if he were taken in," Paula said.

"Maybe he was sick of a god who demanded living sacrifices," Josh countered. "I didn't especially like that Chac-Mool statue at the museum. They put live, still-beating hearts in that plate he holds."

Gayle shook her head at all of them. "Maybe Tutul Xiu—Melchor—encountered the Lord."

No one replied.

What precisely did encountering the Lord mean? Paula wondered as she stepped away from the painting. She watched the worshipers coming and going throughout the cathedral. Did encountering God mean to have a vision? To somehow hear His voice? What was the difference between scoffers and those who believed so devoutly?

As the group left the cathedral, she saw that Gayle was praying. In the vestibule, Paula was strangely moved by the begging cripples and gave all of her coins to them.

Wandering across the street to the plaza with the group, she admired the flowers and hedges as well as the attractive Meridans sitting on beautiful wrought iron benches. Others strolled along the spacious curving sidewalks.

"My turn to take your picture," Josh said to Matt. He directed him and Paula to sit in a white *confidenciale,* an S-curved Victorian loveseat. "And if this one gets published, I earn the ten dollars."

77

Matt laughed as he pulled Paula along to one of the curious concrete seats that looked perfect for quiet and eminently respectable tête-à-têtes. Sitting down, they faced each other, yet were sitting side by side with the S-curve of the loveseat separating them.

Overhead, scattered shafts of sunlight gleamed through the branches and leaves of the sprawling Indian laurel tree, and birds twittered, but she was scarcely aware of them. She saw nothing but Matt's sun-burnished hair, the confident tilt of his square chin, and the blueness of his eyes.

"A little closer," Josh said, looking at them through the camera. "Now how about kissing her, Matt? Only for the picture, of course. I'm sure the *Santa Rosita Times* would like that! A little extra for their money!"

"Men!" Paula said with an embarrassed laugh.

Matt grinned at Josh. "You're embarrassing Paula."

She smiled for the camera, but her back stiffened with resistance as Matt leaned toward her.

"It's not that I don't want to," he whispered, "but I prefer to choose the place and the moment myself."

Her heart skipped as he rested his hand lightly on hers, then there was the click of the camera, and everyone was chattering.

"Will you join me in a carriage ride after lunch?" Matt asked.

Looking into his eyes, she could not resist. "Yes, Matt," she replied, though an inner voice warned against it.

"You're blushing," he murmured.

"It must be the sun," she answered, laughing. She refused to spoil the moment by looking at the others, nor did she care what they thought.

chapter
5

Arriving at the restaurant, Paula was surprised that its atmosphere wasn't rustic. The main dining room exuded richness with its white stucco walls, great curving arches and beautifully carved dark woodwork around the French doors and tall windows. Crystal chandeliers hung from the high ceiling, and oil paintings on the walls gave emphasis to the continental atmosphere. Well-dressed Meridans dined at tables appointed with damask tablecloths, fine china, and shimmering goblets.

Matt looked impressed as they awaited the maître d'. "Except for the arches, it's quite Parisian."

Gayle said, "I've never before seen 'oriental carpets' made of tile!"

"No moths," Josh quipped.

"And probably no haute cuisine," Vanessa commented.

Paula wished that everyone didn't sound so knowledgeable about Paris, oriental rugs, and haute cuisine.

The maître d' arrived and offered them a choice of the air-conditioned indoor elegance or casual courtyard dining under the trees.

"I cast a vote for outside," Gayle said, and everyone agreed except Mrs. Perrota, who finally acquiesced *if* she could have a chair in the shade. It occurred to Paula that Tony would have opted for indoors too; he'd always found elegance terribly important. Now why was she thinking about him? She chided herself as they made their way through the courtyard. She was supposed to be forgetting him.

A white-suited waiter, napkin folded over his arm, seated them at a round table among Moorish arches, black wrought-iron gates, and potted palms. Paula noticed as Matt held the chair for her that Evan was hurrying around to sit on her other side.

Evan smiled warmly. "May I sit beside you?"

"Of course," she replied, aware that Matt was taking note. "Have you two been introduced?"

"Not really," Evan answered.

She nervously performed the introductions, then found herself adding, "Evan and I are old friends."

"So I presumed," Matt said in a curious tone of voice.

Was he jealous? Paula wondered. If that wouldn't be an odd turn of events!

She shifted her attention to the huge embossed menus presented to them. "I can't believe these selections," she remarked to divert their attention. "Garlic soup . . . lime soup . . . tortilla soup . . ."

Gayle said, "For the entrée we're supposed to try *Pibil* chicken. It's baked in banana leaves, as is the pork. They're Yucatan specialties."

"I'll stick with the lobster," Mrs. Perotta stated. Though seated in the shade, she had lowered the brim of her black straw hat so no errant ray of sunshine might possibly touch her face.

Josh chuckled. "I'm looking forward to the mango mousse."

Everyone checked the menus. Mango mousse and carioca crepes were indeed listed among the more mundane desserts.

Amid the good-natured chatter, Paula felt her tensions slowly dissolve. She was not going to think about Tony, nor was she prepared to be a bone of contention between Matt and Evan—she was going to sit back and enjoy the dinner.

A balmy breeze stirred the leaves in the overhead tree, and soft Spanish music floated through the courtyard. Several parties of American tourists sat at distant tables, but many diners chatted in Spanish, German, and French, and the dignified waiters moved quickly about the tables.

"Pleasant, isn't it?" Matt mused aloud.

"It looks like a scene from a travel poster," Paula responded, and they sat quietly sharing the sight. "The kind of picture to store away in our memories."

"Just what I was thinking," Evan said.

Paula turned a bright smile on him. She'd almost forgotten he was there and suspected he'd sensed it. As she recalled his recent divorce, her heart welled with sympathy, and she turned her attention to him.

The waiters served dinner with dignity, and everyone seemed pleased with the food as well as the restaurant's ambience. Paula's *Pibil* pork—chunks of lean pork cooked in banana leaves and seasoned with an unfamiliar red spice—was delectable. Pickled red onion slices, tasting unusually sweet, and thick, wonderfully flavored black beans were equally interesting.

"Another tortilla?" Matt offered, passing the lidded basket of warm corn tortillas around again.

"Just one more," she said. "I've never had any so delicious. I'm going to have to walk off lunch—"

"Don't forget the calesa ride."

She flushed. "I haven't."

"I hope not," he responded with pleasure.

Nonplused by a flurry of emotions, she turned to pass the

tortilla basket to Evan. She was appalled to see the waiter serving him another bottle of Mexican beer—Evan's third or fourth. "Don't you think that's too much . . . ," she began.

Evan had been speaking to the waiter. "Did you say something, Paula?"

"Another . . . another tortilla?" She had no right to criticize him just because she didn't care for alcoholic beverages, she decided. Her grandfather had been an alcoholic, and she and her parents had not cared to discover whether they'd inherited the tendency.

"Yes, thanks," Evan replied. He fumbled to extract a tortilla from the basket, then extolled the virtues of dinner and what they'd seen of Merida.

Paula nodded politely, aware of Matt's interest in her conversation with Evan.

Vanessa had been strangely quiet during the general table conversation, but when they sat back to await dessert, she engaged Matt in a quietly intense conversation. "It wasn't really my fault!" she insisted with annoyance, then looked petulant.

What wasn't her fault? Paula wondered. Something about the calesa ride last night, or about marrying Kurt Packard years ago? Everyone had thought then that Vanessa's jet set husband was quite a catch. Perhaps he'd become bored with her as he had with several prior wives.

Paula turned toward Evan, searching for something to say.

"You're very beautiful, Paula," he said with passion. "Far more beautiful than when we were in school."

"Why, thank you. . . ." The smell of beer on his breath was repulsive, and the tone of his voice reminded her of the way Tony used to compliment her. "No braces now!" she quickly added with a laugh.

He ignored her attempt at humor. "I was a fool not to

pursue you harder, but when I went to college, you were just a junior in high school and you seemed like a kid. I thought I wanted a more . . . you know, a more sophisticated girlfriend. That kind of girl was exciting to me then." He looked embarrassed and grabbed a deep breath. "Well, you know what happened, I suppose."

"I'm sorry, Evan."

"We had a great time at first, but she never wanted to stop partying, even when we were married. Every day was supposed to be fun, fun, fun, and she started hanging around bars—"

"You don't have to tell me, Evan."

He shrugged. "I guess I just wanted to apologize for not seeing how wonderful you'd turn out."

She patted his arm. "Thank you, but I'm not so wonderful. And you don't have to apologize for anything. We had some nice times together when we were teenagers. We were far too young to be serious."

"And now . . . ?" He cast a meaningful glance at Matt.

She was unsure of how to answer and finally said, "Matt and I are old friends too."

She wished that she knew what Matt and Vanessa were discussing so seriously.

Matt joined her at the rear of the group when they left the restaurant. "Who's just old friends?" he asked.

Paula blushed again. "Were you eavesdropping, Matt Montgomery?"

He grinned. "Listening is more like it."

"What should I have told Evan—that you'd been my babysitter?"

"That makes me sound ancient."

"What then?"

His eyes danced with mischief. "You should have said that we're *very* good friends."

"Oh, Matt!"

"Oh, Paula!" he mocked, and they both laughed.

Strange, she thought, sometimes she was nearly tongue-tied around him, yet other times there was this feeling of camaraderie.

Looking down the street at the others, she noticed Vanessa's glare. If only she hadn't come along! This relatively inexpensive tour didn't strike her as the type of traveling Vanessa would favor unless—as Gayle had suggested—she were after Matt again.

Ahead of them, the others stood waiting on the busy street corner for a traffic light to change.

"Let's lose them!" Matt whispered. He grabbed her hand and hurried her across the other street.

They were rushing down the sidewalk when Josh yelled, "Hey, where are you two going?"

"See you later!" Matt called back.

"I didn't realize how full of mischief you are," Paula laughed.

"Only because I was too serious for so many years. Eagle Scout and all. You should know."

"And you're not now?"

"I'm never serious on vacation!"

As they slowed their steps, she was all too aware that he still had her hand. She tried to slip it away, but he pulled it to his lips, kissing her fingertips.

Paula's muscles became fluid; she managed a wry tone. "Just what are you doing, Matt Montgomery?"

"If you don't know . . ." He chuckled. "Certainly you've had your hand kissed before. As I recall, you've been most thoroughly kissed!"

She darted him an embarrassed look. Being so thoroughly kissed by him was part of the trouble, she thought, though she didn't attempt to wrest her hand away again. It felt all too wonderful to hold hands with him; she would have to keep up a light banter and remember that none of this was significant. He'd said himself—perhaps not simply in jest—he wasn't serious while on vacation.

When they reached the edge of the Plaza de la Independencia, he waved for one of the calesas lined up along the street. "Look at that, they've kept the best horse for us!"

"You're right. Some look like they've seen far better days." At least the lively bay pulling the high-wheeled carriage wouldn't make her feel guilty about its plight.

"Buenas tardes," the elderly driver said with a tip of his faded straw hat. He exchanged a few words of English with Matt, making arrangements for the drive through the city.

As the driver helped her up the steps of the shiny black cab, she noted his handsome hawk nose. "Mayan?" she asked.

"Sí," he said proudly. "Maya."

Moments later, she and Matt were seated in the cab's black enclosure and the driver lightly touched the bay's flanks with a length of sisal rope tied to a stick. The horse started off and clippity-clopped down the street in the midst of the light afternoon traffic.

Sitting back, Matt cast a speculative look at her, then slipped his arm around the back of their seat, his fingers cupping her shoulder.

An almost imperceptible shiver fluttered through her. Swallowing hard, she looked out at the city, uncertain of what to do. Surely she'd given away her feelings earlier by allowing him to hold her hand—or he wouldn't have chanced this move.

"I feel as if I've known you forever, yet don't know you," he said. "Do you have the same feeling?"

She nodded, too disconcerted by his nearness to speak. She looked blindly out at the Spanish colonial buildings surrounding the tree-shaded zocalo.

After a while he said, "This is the best way to see a city."

She glanced at him and realized that despite his confident bearing, he was feeling unnerved too. She finally said, "You look like an emperor out surveying his realm."

"I don't know that I'd care for that title. The emperor of Mexico didn't last too long." He took her hand in his. "I think I'd rather be a conquistador!"

She returned his smile uneasily, not certain of his play on words. Suddenly she had the impression that they were being observed. Looking aside, she saw their luncheon group strolling along on the sidewalk. Vanessa's face was rigid with fury.

"We're being watched," Matt said.

"They're going to talk," Paula responded. She tried to extract her hand from his, but he gripped her more firmly and she could hardly put up a struggle with the others watching. To her relief, the horse pulled the calesa into a left turn with the traffic, concealing them behind the carriage's black enclosure.

For a while neither of them spoke. They gazed out at the passing city scene, though Paula felt such a flurry of emotions that she scarcely saw anything.

Matt asked, "Does it matter to you what they might say?"

"In a way . . ." For one thing, she didn't want to be thought a fool; for another, there'd just been Tony.

"Is that why you ran off the night of Dr. Zayere's talk?" Matt asked. "You worried what they'd say?"

"No." How could she possibly say that she'd run because of her certainty he'd prefer Vanessa to her? That all of the years she'd yearned for him, he'd always preferred Vanessa? That she didn't really trust men anymore?

He caught up her hand in his and kissed her fingertips again. "Paula . . ." His blue eyes brimmed with warmth, and he turned her to him, drawing her close so slowly and gently that it afforded her every opportunity to resist.

Trembling against him, she whispered, "Oh, Matt!" Her mouth reached for his. The bare brushing of their lips was cataclysmic, and she shuddered with happiness. As their kiss intensified, she felt a curious sense of old lovers becoming reunited. Matt, oh, Matt! her heart cried out again and again.

When they finally moved apart, he whispered, "Why did it take me so long to find you?"

"I was always there." Her arms circled his neck, her fingers were in his golden hair as she had so often dreamed.

"Paula," he murmured as his lips sought hers again and again. After a while he said, "We'd better catch our breath!"

Her emotions still swirling, she nodded and rested her head against the seat, listening to her heart race. When she opened her eyes, she found him watching her.

"This is the last thing that I expected on this trip," he said. "I hope you don't think . . ." He shook his head. "Here, let me hold your hand, Paula; that seems safe enough."

She said nothing, only looking at him and offering her hand. She didn't want to talk or to think or to worry, only to live in this moment's radiance. Surely he loved her. Surely he must.

They sat hand in hand as the calesa moved through the city, then down the tree-lined Paseo de Montejo, where they'd ridden in the morning on the bus, past the great pink monument, then back around the corner by the Museum of Anthropology. Thank goodness she'd taken notes earlier, for she wouldn't be able to now.

Far too soon their ride was over, and they returned to the Plaza de la Independencia. Matt helped her down from the calesa, and she looked about to see if Vanessa and the others were nearby. There were only Meridians and other tourists.

The driver nodded pleasantly at them as he drove away, and she wondered how many loveswept couples he'd carried behind him in his lifetime.

"What would you like to do for the rest of the afternoon?" Matt asked.

Take another carriage ride, she was tempted to say, but she resisted. "Sit in the zocalo for a while," she answered instead. "I need to work on my notes . . . to describe the park and the buildings, to get the feel of the city and the people."

"And I need more pictures," he said. Readying his camera, he noticed a group of Mayan women walking by in their white huipils, and he snapped pictures of them. Other Meridan women in Western dress strolled by with their families. "They're supposed to be the most beautiful women in Mexico," he remarked.

She felt a ridiculous stab of jealousy. It was bad enough that he attracted women with his good looks—glances by the dark-eyed beauties made it clear they found the tall, blue-eyed, blond American appealing—she didn't have to make it worse by being jealous. Being with Matt would always be like this.

The afternoon slipped by, and suddenly the sun's rays slanted low through the plaza's trees. Returning to the hotel, they stopped at the colorful shops, and she bought a white guayabera shirt for her father and hand-embroidered caftans—a pink one for her mother, a blue for herself. Matt purchased an antique churchyard bell. "For my house or condo or whatever," he said. "It looks like just the thing for over a patio gate."

He didn't seem like a man with nesting instincts, Paula thought, but then his interest in photography had surprised her too.

As they approached their hotel, he slipped an arm around her shoulders and gave her a fast squeeze. "It's been a wonderful afternoon for me, Paula."

She smiled at him, her heart reaching up beyond her eyes as she remembered their kisses and now their comfortable companionship. "For me too."

He dropped a kiss on her hair. "How about tonight? Do you want to go to the mariachi restaurant?"

"I'd love to. All you have to say is mariachi music, and I'm ready to go."

His hotel room was just down the hallway from hers and, as he dropped her off, he glanced briefly around. "There's no one," he murmured and tilted her chin up to him. His mouth, warm and exciting, touched her forehead, her eyelids, the tip of her nose, until his lips found her mouth in a kiss that sent tremors racing through her again.

For a second, a treacherous second, she hesitated, not really wanting to resist, but knew that she must. "Matt!" she demurred softly, pulling away.

He stepped back. "Six-thirty?" he asked. "That should give us time to clean up and change."

"Six-thirty," she agreed. She unlocked her door and, smiling at him, finally closed it behind her. Inside the room, she leaned back against the door, her eyes closed. How could all of this be happening when she had been so determined not to fall in love again? And how could she *not* love Matt now, when she had for so many years!

"Did you and Matt have a nice afternoon?" Gayle asked as she and Paula finished dressing for the evening.

"Yes, very nice," Paula responded, busying herself inordinately with pulling on her navy blue high-heeled sandals. She hoped that Gayle wouldn't pursue the subject, and fortunately she didn't.

Paula stood up, the silk of her royal blue dress smooth under her fingers as she stepped to the mirror. Not only did the royal blue color of the shirtwaist dress enhance the blue-green of her eyes, but her entire face seemed aglow with happiness. Her honey-blond hair was parted on the side, the bangs brushed off her face, and casual waves curved almost to her shoulders. For once, she looked exactly as she wanted to.

Moments later Matt and Josh knocked at the door. "We have over an hour," Matt said. "The reservations are for eight o'clock at the restaurant."

How marvelous he looks in his light tan resort suit, Paula thought. She grabbed her navy clutch bag from the bed. "Maybe we can sit in the plaza and listen to the music. There are band concerts on Sunday nights."

"Sounds like a good idea," Matt said. "Even without music, it's one of the most interesting plazas I've seen anywhere."

"I'm thirsty," Gayle remarked on the way downstairs, and they decided to stop first at the hotel's refreshment bar out on the marble terrace.

"Isn't this lovely?" Paula asked as Matt seated her at a table near the white balustrade. The terrace overlooked an extensive walled garden in which water trickled over an elegant fountain; purple bougainvillaea spilled over the trellised walls. In the distance, an artist sketched the sprawling hotel's graceful arches.

"You're lovely," Matt said, and she knew he meant it. Perhaps she wasn't as strikingly beautiful as Vanessa, but at the moment he found her appealing; the thought gave her exquisite joy.

"Mosquitoes!" Gayle brushed one from her arm. "I think I'd rather go to the coffee shop."

"How about you, Paula?" Matt asked.

A soft breeze wafted through the balmy air and the garden

was magnificent. "I prefer it here." Besides, much as she liked Gayle and Josh, she wanted to be alone with Matt.

Gayle turned a wry look on Paula.

"See you two at dinner," Josh said as he and Gayle left.

Later, when Paula and Matt sat on a park bench on the downtown plaza, Paula's legs and the back of her neck began to itch. She thought there might be mosquitoes, but she didn't see any.

"Those invisible mosquitoes must find you delicious," Matt observed. "Maybe we'd better walk."

They strolled along the crowded sidewalks hand in hand. It appeared that all of the Meridan families had dressed up for the evening and were out promenading through the plaza. There was an aura of contentment and friendliness about them, as well as a natural dignity in their attire and demeanor. By comparison, most of the passing tourists were unattractive in their skimpy clothing.

On one end of the plaza near the bandstand, workers were setting up wooden folding chairs.

"When does the music begin?" Paula asked in her imperfect Spanish.

"A las ocho," one of the men responded with a polite nod.

"Eight o'clock," she told Matt.

"We'll miss it. Too bad."

Still it was wonderful to stroll with him and to watch the young children happily chase soap bubbles through the air. Nearby a vendor sold liquid and wands for blowing bubbles. Another dealt in bright plastic balls on strings. Other vendors offered popcorn, ice cream, flat sugar candies with nuts, tortilla chips with a sauce shaken into the plastic bags. One vendor's wares perplexed them; he dispensed small packets from two large pouches hanging on either side of him, each suspended from the cloth hung over his neck. Customers crowded around, and he was always just far enough away that his wares were a mystery.

"Peanuts!" Matt said at last with a chuckle. "He's selling peanuts. Would you like some?"

"I'd love some. I'm starving."

As they sat down again to shell and eat the peanuts, she thought she felt more mosquitoes. Yet what did a few bites matter when she could share a park bench with Matt?

When it was time to leave, schoolchildren wearing band uniforms and carrying musical instruments assembled near the bandstand. "If only we could stay for the music!" she wished.

"My sentiments exactly," Matt agreed. "If I ever do the photography books, it won't be while taking fast tours like this one. I'd probably want to spend at least a whole week on a city like Merida. There's a sense of pride and of the universality of life here, especially in this plaza."

"I know just what you mean. It's like watching the rites of passage." There were courting couples, newlyweds, pregnant women with their husbands, mothers nursing infants, fathers pushing babies in carriages, families with well-mannered children accompanying them, and beaming grandparents. How content they appeared to be!

As they departed, she reminded herself that her happiness came from being with Matt. Surely it would not have been so wonderful without him at her side.

The mariachi restaurant was only a few blocks past their hotel, and they arrived promptly at eight, meeting Gayle and Josh just inside the entrance.

"Buenas noches," the ebullient maître d' said in greeting. They responded with a hearty "Buenas noches!"

"Santa Rosita party," Matt explained.

"Of course! You will follow me, por favor?" He led them

swiftly through the dimly lit, cavernous restaurant to a large table next to the dance floor.

Vanessa, wearing a low-cut red silk dress, sat conversing with her mother and five or six others. "There you are, Matt," Vanessa exclaimed. "Do come sit with me."

Matt faltered in his stride, and Paula was so stunned at the woman's gall that she could think of nothing to say. From the corner of her eye she saw Gayle and Josh arriving just in time to take in the entire scene.

Before anyone could stop him, Josh blithely appropriated the chair next to Vanessa as if he had not overheard the interchange.

Bless him, Paula thought in relief while the maître d' seated her and Matt some distance away.

Moments later, Evan and his friends arrived at the table. "Buenas noches, señorita," he said with an accent even more atrocious than her own. "May I have the honor of sitting next to you again?"

"I don't know about the *honor*," she responded with a laugh, "but I'd be pleased to sit with you." She hoped that he wouldn't be upset by the romantic attachment that had developed between her and Matt, particularly since their escape from the rest of them after lunch.

Others from the Santa Rosita group arrived. Finally there were sixteen at the rectangular table, everyone sharing his or her afternoon's adventures.

"We have ringside seats," Matt remarked.

"Yes, we certainly do." Paula couldn't conceive of anything less than ringside seats after how wonderful the entire day had been. She sat enthralled with happiness. It seemed that words were unessential between them now, that she could spend a lifetime simply basking in his presence.

She looked about the mariachi restaurant. A wrought-iron

railing beside them separated the capacious dining area from the lowered dance floor, and beyond there was a raised stage for the evening's entertainment.

Matt caught her hand in his. "What a wonderful day it's been."

"For me too." She remembered the bliss of being in his arms and thought he was recalling it now as well.

"A nice table," Evan Walker commented on the other side of her.

It took her a moment to respond. "Yes, it is." From the corner of her eye, she glimpsed Matt smiling at her, then the waiter presented their menus.

The selections were as tempting as those at the restaurant where they had eaten lunch. "Would you like to share portions of the entrées with me?" Matt asked.

"A wonderful idea! I've been eyeing chicken mole and hot green enchiladas and Yucatan beef tips—"

Matt gave a chuckle. "Let's have all three."

"You're joking," she protested, then noticing how low the prices were, she agreed.

The busboys brought *bolillos,* freshly baked rolls whose delicious aroma preceded them, as well as bottles of mineral water. Nearby tables in the enormous restaurant filled rapidly. The evening was so alive with chatter and laughter that it seemed only minutes before their waiter brought their green enchiladas covered with a melted cheese sauce.

"Looks marvelous," Paula said before trying her first forkful. The fiery pepper burned her tongue, yet it didn't deter her from eating more until suddenly her mouth felt afire.

Matt laughed as she wildly reached for her glass of mineral water and held the cooling liquid in her mouth. "It creeps up on you, doesn't it?"

She sent him a sidelong glance. Just like you do, she thought.

"And what did that look mean?" Matt asked.

As if he didn't know! His blue eyes were so compelling and his smile so dazzling that she knew she could never resist him.

Occasionally Evan turned to her from his friends for small talk, but he evidently noticed the magnetism between her and Matt, and was carefully polite.

They feasted on chicken mole—roasted chicken covered with a chocolate sauce—and Mexican beef tips cooked with sweet peppers and onions. Again there was a scoop of the delicious black beans. When she could eat no more, she sat back contently. Happiness surged through her as she observed Matt finish his dinner, relishing every bite. He ate with gusto and enjoyment, yet with every sign of refinement. It seemed that he did everything pleasantly.

As the waiter served coffee, busloads of tourists streamed into the restaurant, filling the enormous room to capacity. After everyone had been given a drink, the house lights dimmed.

Spirited mariachi music swirled from the darkness, then a spotlight hit the stage. Golden instrument glistening, the trumpeter led the group in the melodious strains of "Guadalahara." The silvery braid on the mariachis' short black jackets, tight charro pants, and sombreros shimmered in the light.

Although she'd often heard mariachi music, tonight it seemed especially delightful as she clapped to the exciting rhythms with the rest of the crowd. She discovered Matt watching her. "I'm so glad we've come. Aren't they wonderful?"

"You make it wonderful," he murmured, his breath warm in her hair.

Later, a troupe of dancers—three couples in brilliantly

colored Mayan costumes—performed the ancient religious dances of their ancestors, worshiping the sun. The bronzed men wore little on their torsos except short skirtlike kirtles, wide collars, and high headdresses decorated with plumes. The women danced in diaphanous costumes with feathers in their hair.

"There's an ancient Egyptian feeling to it," Matt observed. Paula laughed. "Exotic, whatever it is."

Next the troupe stamped and whirled through contemporary Mayan folk dances, the women in white embroidered huipils, the men in white muslin peon costumes. They changed costumes with lightning speed while the mariachis played. Their repertoire included everything from dignified Spanish dances to comic bullfights, ending with an exuberant Mexican hat dance around huge sombreros.

Later a marimba band of nine men wearing amusing folkloric costumes captured the audience's enthusiasm and often their laughter, especially with a comic cock fight.

"There's a childlike joy to the marimba music," Paula remarked.

Matt nodded, as caught up in the music as she. "They love playing it so much that we can't help liking it too."

Yet not everyone delighted in it. And certainly Tony would have found it childish. Suddenly it seemed impossible to imagine why she'd ever fallen in love with him. Perhaps it had been partly out of loneliness in Phoenix.

She looked away, trying to redirect her thoughts. At her side, Evan looked only vaguely interested in the marimba band and was polishing off a third or fourth decanter of the house wine with his friends. Down the table, Vanessa looked bored. What was the difference between those who delighted in the joy of the music—and life—and those who were disinterested? The answer probably had little to do with being terribly knowledgeable about either.

When the show ended, a small orchestra played Latin dance music, and couples from the audience made their way to the floor. Paula turned to Matt, only to find Vanessa approaching him.

"Aren't you going to ask me to dance?" she inquired. "I remember we used to do a very exciting tango after taking those dancing lessons."

Paula looked away.

"Enjoying the evening?" Evan asked from the other side of Paula, his breath reeking of alcohol.

She nodded mutely. It had been wonderful until now. Evan was saying something about the gourd being used as a musical instrument. On her other side, she was aware of Matt excusing himself, rising, and walking away with Vanessa. After a while, she heard nothing of what Evan was saying, only the sensuous rhythms of "Tango of Love." She glanced toward the dance floor.

Couples moved smoothly across the floor with stylistic posturings to the exotic Latin music, capturing the audience's attention. The passion of the dance pervaded the room, quickly stilling conversation at the tables until only the sensuous music vibrated in the air. When the song neared its conclusion, dancers stopped, one couple after another, catching their breath and standing aside to admire the most sensational dancers.

Two of the couples—middle-aged and accustomed to each other's every move—were exquisite, but the most ravishing twosome on the floor was Matt and Vanessa. They exceeded Paula's worst expectations, dancing to the exaggerated rhythm with their eyes locked in passionate interchange. Vanessa was unbelievably voluptuous in her red crepe dress, and Matt, his tan suit almost white under the dim lights, held her waist in a firm grip as they executed their turns.

97

Everyone at the table watched them, several directing curious glances at Paula.

"Know what they're doing, don't they?" Evan asked.

Paula didn't respond, unable to take her eyes from them. They knew exactly what they were doing, Matt as much as Vanessa, and there was far more to their performance than the intricacies of the steps. It was the entanglement of their lives for years—an entangled tango of passion and lingering love. The Latin music throbbed on and on. With the expertise of professional dancers, Matt and Vanessa moved to the precise rhythm, erect and cheek to cheek, then shifted direction with stunning precision.

The long slits in the slim skirt of Vanessa's red silk dress displayed her lovely long legs. Their gaze locked with such passion that it radiated all around them. At the music's tempestuous last notes, Matt dipped Vanessa deeply and masterfully. Vanessa's hand, at the back of Matt's neck, pulled his face down to hers and for an instant their lips met and held.

The audience and other dancers burst into applause, and Paula swung away, her eyes shut for an unendurable moment.

"Do you want me to take you back to the hotel?" Evan asked quietly.

She nodded, afraid to open her eyes for fear the tears would come. What a terrible fool she had been again!

"Let's go then," he said.

In seconds she was up and weaving through the crowded tables for the other end of the room. She wondered what Matt might think of her leaving, but when she glanced at the dance floor, he and Vanessa were dancing an encore.

"Don't run!" Evan said behind her. He caught her by the shoulder and she slowed. Whatever she did, she must not run, Paula told herself over and over. She'd already made enough of a spectacle of herself.

"He's a playboy, Paula," Evan said, opening the door for her. "People like you and me get hurt when we take playboys and playgirls too seriously."

She caught back a sob and shook her head. It wasn't as if she hadn't known better, as if she hadn't been warned about Matt! But why did the warnings have to be so painfully true?

chapter
6

THE NEXT MORNING PAULA CALLED room service while Gayle showered. Under no circumstances was she going to face Matt over breakfast, Paula thought in anguish. Besides her heartache about Matt's passionate tango and public kiss with Vanessa, irritating red welts from mosquito bites had risen on her arms and legs—mementos of her romantic interlude with him in the plaza. Worse, her upper lip itched as if a welt might rise there too. At the moment, the only saving grace she could think of was that Evan had been a perfect gentleman when he brought her home.

"Aren't you going downstairs for breakfast?" Gayle asked when she was dressed.

Paula, still in her blue nightgown and peignoir, shook her head. "I just can't seem to get organized this morning, so I've called room service."

Gayle raised an eyebrow at her, but said nothing.

"I'll be out for the bus in time, don't worry."

"Am I that much of a mother hen?"

"Not really," Paula admitted. "Only a caring friend."

"Thanks." Gayle's smile suddenly went awry as she looked at Paula. "I just wish Matt weren't so wealthy and handsome!"

Paula tried to brush her hair nonchalantly. "Why do you say that?"

Gayle grabbed her purse and headed for the door. "Because then Vanessa wouldn't be interested in him!"

As the door closed, Paula sank down on her bed. What Gayle said was true. But was Matt aware of it? In any case, it was senseless to ruin the day over last night; it had been difficult enough to sleep.

Onward and forward, she finally reminded herself and stood up forlornly. She plodded to her closet and selected white culottes and a scooped-neck, cap-sleeved lavender blouse as appropriate for climbing the Mayan pyramids at Uxmal.

A knock sounded at the door. "Room service."

Paula opened the door. It was a white-uniformed bellboy with her breakfast tray, and she let him in.

As he headed for the round table and chairs by the window, there was another knock at the still ajar door.

"Paula?"

The sound of Matt's voice caused a tremor to flutter through her. She turned, but he hadn't stepped in. "Just a minute." She quickly tipped the bellboy and went with him to the door. "Yes?" she asked.

He wore a regretful expression. "Gayle said you weren't coming down for breakfast, and I wanted to talk to you."

Paula said nothing, focusing on his pale blue shirt collar to avoid his eyes.

"About last night. I'm sorry. I know how it must have looked. . . ."

Her heart hardened. She had forgiven Tony again and again; she had decided yesterday morning at breakfast that maybe Matt's escorting Vanessa on the calesa ride meant nothing. And *now* she was to pretend that the tempestuous tango and kiss were meaningless too! "Oh, Matt!" she blurted, "I didn't really believe that you were such a . . .' The word *fool* was on the tip of her tongue.

"A what?" he asked with an unreadable expression.

She bit her lower lip to stop its trembling.

People passed by in the hallway and glanced at them.

"Look—can't I come in for a minute?"

"I'm not dressed," she stated flatly.

"Paula! The bellboy was in there. . . ."

She glanced down at the blue lacy peignoir covering her nightgown.

"I promise not to touch you," Matt said.

She opened the door. "Just for a minute."

He stepped in. "Paula, I just wanted to . . ." He tried valiantly to keep his eyes on her face. "I just wanted to try to explain that Vanessa asked me to dance and she's the one who pulled my head down to kiss her when I couldn't possibly let go in that dip." He stopped, and his eyes roamed over her. He said abruptly, "Don't you ever let another man in here, bellboy or not!"

"How dare you tell me what to do!"

"Paula!" he whispered hoarsely, sweeping her into his arms.

Be careful! her mind flashed, but his mouth was suddenly warm on hers again and her strength seeped away as she began to give in to his fervent kiss. When she found her arms moving involuntarily around his neck, reason asserted itself with a vengeance, and she wrenched her lips from his. "Get out of here, Matt, go away . . . !"

He looked guilty and backed to the door.

Angrily she opened it. "There's no need for you to make excuses! But I really did trust you when I let you kiss me in the calesa. I didn't want to believe that it was a mere . . . hobby for you."

"A hobby! Where did you ever—"

"Moreover you promised not to touch me in here!" she

called out behind him, not caring who might hear. "Now go, please!" She shut the door firmly and turned away. Why hadn't he left her alone? He'd only made things immeasurably worse! It was bad enough to be so attracted to him. She wished she could cry, but her heart ached too horribly for tears.

She stood in the middle of the room in utter desolation. How could she possibly handle being with him day after day the rest of the week? It didn't seem humanly possible to cope with this situation. Worse, the trip had barely begun.

Finally she threw on her clothes. As she pulled on her white sandals, an answer began to come to her. Perhaps . . . perhaps Evan wouldn't mind helping. He would understand since he'd been so badly hurt by love too.

Making her decision, she picked up the telephone.

Paula delayed long enough to be one of the last passengers boarding the bus. When she climbed on, she immediately saw Evan. Not only had he saved her a seat as she had requested, but the front one.

"I thought you'd want to see out as well as possible for taking notes," he explained, standing up as she pressed past him to the window seat.

"Thanks." She sat down. "It's perfect."

Moments later, the driver shut the bus door and pulled out into traffic.

Jacob manned the microphone. "Buenos días," he said with his now familiar drowsy smile. "Today we will drive to the Mayan ruins of Uxmal and Kabah, but first we will stop at a local bank since many of you wish to change travelers' checks."

Paula pulled out her notebook and pencil, and looked around. Outside, the streets were jammed with cars, and on the sidewalks, housewives carried mesh bags full of tomatoes, oranges, and papayas. She forced herself to take notes.

"There we have a bread seller," Jacob said, pointing out the elderly man on a motorcycle with an enormous metal container in back. "And there is the mail carrier on his bicycle." They seemed oblivious to the roaring traffic all around them.

Within minutes, the bus parked in front of the bank, a modern marble building on the fashionable Paseo de Montejo. Paula left her notebook on the seat, and hurried out hoping to avoid Matt, wishing she'd never have to face him again.

In the bank Jacob led them to the proper line, where she and Evan quickly exchanged their travelers' checks. As they walked out, she glimpsed Matt and Vanessa together toward the end of the line. He was slightly turned away, chuckling about something. How dare he! After acting so innocent this morning! If he didn't care for Vanessa, why was he always in her vicinity?

When Paula stepped out into the sunshine, an unshaven mail carrier—identifiable by his billed hat and the mailbag over his shoulder—was blowing a whistle to hold back traffic. Their bus backed up slightly. In front of it, a woman extracted her compact car from the tight parking space.

"What on earth?" Paula exclaimed.

"He's angling for a tip," Evan said, amused. "Just watch."

Moments later, when the woman had her car out, she presented a bill to the mail carrier, who bowed most respectfully to hide his grin.

"I have a feeling that this is *his* street," Evan chuckled.

They stood in the dappled sunshine and early morning breeze, watching the mail carrier needlessly direct another car from its parking space. This time he was tipped with a cigarette.

"They must be at his mercy," Evan said. "It looks like blackmail."

"What's that over there?" someone asked.

Paula looked toward a vendor in the shade. His bicycle had been transformed into a stand with an ice box and a tray for holding assorted syrup bottles. As she and Evan approached, the elderly Mexican nodded politely and continued to shave ice from a huge block in the metal ice box.

This was just the local color that a travel article needed, Paula thought despite her despair. "What is this for?" she asked the vendor in her best Spanish.

He answered in the incomprehensible Mayan dialect. Seconds later, the mail carrier was behind them handling the translation.

"It's for selling ices," Evan explained. "He asks if we want to buy some."

"Not this early in the morning!" she responded.

Evan persevered in Spanish. The ices vendor nodded, and the mail carrier grinned. Others from their group gathered to see what was going on.

The ices man demonstrated step by step how he made his product. He shaved slivers from the chunk of ice in the box, placed the shaved ice into a plastic glass and added a syrup smelling like banana, then gave it to the mail carrier who doffed his hat in thanks before taking his first sip.

Evan produced a bill from his pocket for the vendor, who nodded with pleasure. But the mail carrier held his hand out for money too

"A wily fellow," Evan chuckled, handing the mail carrier a bill too. "That wasn't in the deal."

"I wonder if they stage that every day when tourist buses stop here at the bank?" Paula mused aloud. The episode had at least diverted her somewhat from her agony.

"You know the old saying," Evan said. "The fox has only one trick, but it's a good one."

She smiled. At least Evan was in a good humor. Looking

up, she saw Matt approaching to take a picture of them with the mail carrier and the ices vendor.

"A good local color shot," he remarked to her.

"Yes," she responded in her coolest tone.

Matt's gaze stopped at her mouth.

She touched a finger to her upper lip, realizing how swollen it was now. Did he think that he'd bruised her with this morning's fervent kiss? Well, let him think what he pleased! It was just a mosquito bite—a reminder of yesterday's stupidity!

She headed back with Evan for the bus. At least he could be entertaining in even the most ordinary circumstances such as buying an ice for the local mail carrier. It would probably never have occurred to Matt to do anything like that.

"Is that a mosquito bite?" Evan asked as they sat down in the bus.

She pulled out a tiny mirror from her handbag and glanced at her reflection. "It certainly looks like it," she said. And it certainly is ugly, she thought, feeling even more glum.

"You're still pretty," Evan said softly, and when she looked up into his brown eyes, she knew he meant it.

"Thanks," she said. At least he seemed to care.

As they drove out of town, Paula made notes about the passing scenery: *new industrial area near Merida's airport, enormous cement factories, a Pemex Oil facility, fields of gray-green sisal hemp plants.*

"Looks like yucca," Evan commented. "A peculiar plant for a crop."

"Yet fortunes were made on it," Paula said, remembering from her research. "At one time, the Yucatan had the world's only supply of the fiber."

When the bus slowed in a village, there were Mayan women walking alongside the street nursing their babies. Several men carried huge bundles of thatch on their backs.

Paula studied the typical native houses with curiosity. They were just ovals of white stucco with roofs of palm fronds, simple but graceful. Some had blue doors, and most were surrounded by widely spaced acacia poles serving as fences. Insubstantial as the fences looked, they kept the pigs in and only a few turkeys wandered along the road.

Beyond the village, the countryside was greener and surprisingly flat in all directions. It was not as jungly as Paula had expected, but it appeared inhospitable—a rough, harsh land with low-growing trees and undergrowth. Despite the moisture in the air, it all looked arid.

Later they drove through a hacienda—one of the grand old estates enclosed by stone fences. "Since our land reform in 1924, this hacienda belongs to the people," Jacob explained over the microphone.

"Doesn't look like their methods have been updated since 1924 either," Evan said with irritation. He pointed out a donkey pulling a load of sisal along the old hacienda's narrow-gauge railway track, a group of Yucatecs trailing behind it. "Everything is still done by hand. Peon labor."

"No computers," Paula joked, hoping to diffuse his sudden change of mood. It appeared that anger lurked just beneath the surface—from his divorce, no doubt.

"Right. No computers," he answered, finally managing a smile.

As they drove through towns and villages there were open air markets with colorful fruits: bananas, watermelon, papaya. And always the lovely thatch-roofed houses, beautiful brown babies, the women in their embroidered white huipils, the men wearing guayabera shirts.

In the countryside, their bus was usually the only vehicle on the white limestone road that cut through the low green vegetation. Finally the land became hilly and the greenery more dense.

"Low jungle," Jacob called it. He launched into a discussion of their destination. "Uxmel is called 'the sublimity of Mayan architecture.' It is one of the most successful architectural achievements of Mayan civilization and is noted for the symmetry and proportions of its buildings," he said. "Uxmal reached its peak in the last half of the Classic Period—A.D. 600 to 900. From the tenth century on it suffered the gradual decline that was the fate of all centers of Mayan culture under foreign conquerors."

Despite Jacob's best efforts, Paula was entirely unprepared for the first awesome view of Uxmal as they rounded a curve in the road. A great white pyramid rose above the low jungle like a majestic phantom from the past.

"There it is!" she exclaimed with nearly everyone else on the bus, knowing that she was not going to be disappointed. "The Temple of the Magician!"

Climbing off the bus, she excitedly joined Jacob and the others near the great cistern where water had been stored thousands of years ago. Even in the shade of the trees, the air was humid, but not nearly as hot as Jacob had warned, since the day was cloudy.

It was difficult to believe that she actually stood where the ancient Mayans had once walked. As she looked away from the towering temple, she saw Matt striding toward her, camera around his neck, blond hair shimmering in the sunshine.

"Don't you think that we should work on this together?" he asked evenly.

She was tempted to say she didn't care whether they sold the articles or not, but that was childish. "Yes, of course we should," she responded in her most businesslike manner.

"What happened to your lip?" he asked oddly, as if he thought he might have bruised it with this morning's kiss.

"Mosquito bite," she replied, turning her attention to Jacob's talk. It was all she could do to concentrate on it.

After he had expounded upon the white limestone Temple of the Magician towering before them like a ziggurat, Jacob said, "Okay, climbers, climb!"

Paula looked up, trying to ignore the pyramid's steepness and noble proportions. She didn't like heights, but a travel writer should climb up to report the view. She started for the pyramid.

"You're going to climb it?" Evan asked.

"I guess so."

He shook his head in disbelief. "Not me!"

She glimpsed Matt stepping away from Vanessa and her mother, and heading for the pyramid's steps too.

"Looks like only a few of us are going to try it," he said. He gestured toward the heavy iron chain anchored to the worn stone steps. "After you."

Paula stuffed the notebook in her shoulder bag, which she then hung around her neck. "Thanks."

She decided not to use the heavy chain since the few tourists climbing down were helping themselves along holding it. She started up the pyramid. The crumbling limestone steps were amazingly narrow, perhaps only five inches wide. Like everyone else, she placed her feet sideways to make her way up the stairway, holding the chalky steps above for balance. After several minutes, she paused to catch her breath and to assess her progress.

Looking down, her stomach lurched wildly at the steepness. She stood rooted in place.

"Hang on to the chain," Matt warned from just below her. "And don't look back."

"Thank you, but I can manage just fine!" she retorted. She'd have to mention in her article that Mayan pyramid climbing was not for everyone. She climbed on, angling toward the heavy chain, then holding onto it as she moved upward.

After a while she stopped for a momentary rest, noticing how far above the trees she'd climbed. Her stomach lurched again. She mounted the next step, then another, moving higher and higher on the seemingly endless staircase. The ancient steps were chalky and uneven, and she was increasingly grateful for the rusty chain and the thick plastic treads under her white sandals.

Finally reaching the top of the pyramid, she stood up with trepidation in the balmy breeze. In the distance the hilly low jungle looked like a green velvet backdrop for the magnificent gray limestone pyramids and other ruins all around. It seemed as if she had climbed into an ancient land, another civilization just below the gray clouds. It was the most magnificent sight she'd ever seen.

"You all right?" Matt asked as he ascended to the pyramid's top with her.

"Just fine," she insisted, although she felt dizzy when she realized there was no sign of steps beyond Matt. The pyramid was so steep that it appeared as if they were on a sky platform with no means of returning.

"You look pale," he remarked, walking to her.

They were alone; there was no way to avoid him. "I'm just fine!"

"Paula, I'm sorry about this morning. It's just that you looked so . . . beautiful, so inviting . . . as you do now."

Her head reeled as she backed away.

He grabbed her arm. "Paula! You'll kill yourself!"

"Then let go of me," she remonstrated, prying his hand from her arm.

Another climber stepped out on top with them, staring at them curiously, then there were more tourists, and Matt moved away.

She sat down as far away as possible from the pyramid's edges, and dug out her notebook to jot down impressions, her heart still hammering over their encounter. He'd no doubt have been delighted to kiss her up here in the sky, swollen lip and all! Perhaps it would be a first for him—kissing someone on top of a Mayan pyramid. Certainly a unique addition to his list.

Calming herself, she began to make notes about the surrounding ruins, familiar now from her research. She was relieved to see that Matt was taking pictures.

To the left, there was a group of Mayan structures, misnamed the Quadrangle of the Nunnery by the conquistadors because of the many cell-like chambers. Nearby was the ancient ball court—site of Mayan religious games. And there were the majestic Palace of the Governor, the House of the Turtles, and the House of the Doves. Tourists wandering among the vast expanses of ruins were mere flecks of color below, and in the distance over the low green jungle were the ruins of another ancient Mayan city, Kabah.

Matt shot pictures in all directions, then sat down beside her. Looking out toward the ruins he quoted, "The white stones of the dead and holy cities that stand now in solitude across the broad land of the Mayab."

"You've read 'The Land of the Pheasant and the Deer,'" she commented. It was from the contemporary lyrical work of the Yucatan's most illustrious literary son, Antonio Mediz Bolio.

"You're not the only one who did some research."

"I'm glad to hear it," she returned.

Josh and others from the Santa Rosita group stepped onto the top. "I couldn't get Gayle to climb up here for anything," Josh said, amazed to see Paula.

"Paula's a regular mountain goat," Matt replied with a chuckle.

She shot him a furious glance since Josh had moved on to see the views.

"Ready to climb down?" Matt asked, unperturbed.

The longer she delayed, the more she would dread it, she told herself. "Ready."

"You're pale again."

"Never mind!" She swallowed hard and headed for the edge where the steps should be. There was only the narrow top step—and seemingly nothing but air below it! She backed away.

"I'll go first," Matt offered.

"Do you think I'll fall on top of you?" she snapped.

He chuckled. "Don't worry. I won't let you fall far."

"No, I don't suppose you would."

Smiling ruefully, he began his descent hanging onto the chain. "I didn't realize how feisty you could be. Anyhow, I *am* sorry."

He was so sorry that he'd immediately headed for Vanessa! she thought.

As she edged toward the first step, she was all too aware of him just below her. She would make it down alone, just to show him if nothing else!

"One step at a time," he cautioned.

Horrified, she kept her eyes on the steps and Matt moving steadily down the pyramid just below her as she grabbed the chain. She would never ever climb a pyramid again, she told herself as she began the slow descent. Each foot shook violently as it reached below for the next well-worn step; she was covered with perspiration despite the overcast sky.

As they moved down the pyramid, hanging onto the iron chain, she knew that Matt was climbing slowly for her benefit.

"Careful here," he warned where more limestone had chalked off.

It seemed forever until she reached the bottom of the steps and stood gratefully on the ground, her legs trembling.

"I think you have a touch of vertigo," he said with amusement.

She darted him a furious look and started for the path leading through the ruins. How dare he find her terror humorous! He probably thought that their romantic interlude had been too!

She made her way silently through the ruins among wildflowers and grasses. Their group had moved on, and she and Matt hurried along to catch up, taking notes and pictures as they went. She'd finally calmed down when they joined their group by the ruin of the Palace of the Governor. Avoiding Matt, she took notes about its stone frieze composed of thousands of tiny pieces fitted together to form images of serpents, latticework, thrones, huts, and columns.

"How was the climb?" Evan asked when she'd finished.

"Wonderful," she answered, ignoring Matt's grin. "I'm sure that Matt has some fantastic pictures."

As they moved along to the hundreds of unexcavated ruins among the weeds and wildflowers, both Matt and Evan stayed at her side, occasionally eyeing each other.

They stepped through a unique corbeled arch and into a blackened room where the ancients had once lived. "How will I ever describe a corbeled arch?" Paula asked Evan.

"Say they're inverted V's with short wooden lintels on top," he suggested.

Matt busied himself taking photos through the arch. As they moved outside again, he focused on the ruins the low jungle was quickly reclaiming.

Vanessa spied him. "There you are, Matt! Would you like me to pose for you by the ruins?"

"Certainly," he answered. "Who could resist such an offer?"

Certainly not Matt! Paula thought. Vanessa was as strikingly sensual as usual in scanty white shorts and a low-cut white T-shirt. No one would even notice the unique arch in the pictures.

Paula was glad to leave them behind and to capture the

flavor of the ancient site in her notes. She rejoined Jacob and the group.

"For centuries the local Mayans have tried to keep the cities of their ancestors secret," Jacob said. "They did not want to disturb the past. Once the digging began, skeletons of the ancient nobility were found inside the pyramids. There were also skeletons found in great clay jars in the fetal position, some buried with their dogs since dogs were thought to lead the way to paradise. And some partially decomposed bodies with their lips sewn so they wouldn't whisper and disturb the living."

Mrs. Perotta waved her hand in disgust. "We don't need to hear about that."

"Older people prefer not to hear about death," Evan murmured.

"I'm not sure it's only older people," Paula responded, considering her own mixed feelings. "My grandparents didn't seem at all frightened. They believed in heaven—in another life beyond death."

"Do you?" he asked seriously.

"I used to. It made life a lot simpler and death a lot easier. But I don't know anymore."

"I think it's all nonsense," he replied. "Science has disproved religion time and time again."

She recalled reading that it was only the biased interpretation of science that could "disprove religion," but she did not feel like discussing it now. She moved on with the group.

The sun beamed through the gray clouds, creating a pinkish glow on the ancient ruins. How magnificent it had once been here. Where had the people gone to? And why? According to Jacob, there were no real answers. Only speculation that they had worn out the land, or been driven away by a warlike tribe, or revolted against the priests and nobility who held the secrets of their culture.

All too soon the group had circled through the extensive ruins and back to the Pyramid of the Magician.

"Time to leave," Jacob said, and they headed reluctantly for the parking lot where the bus waited.

Paula stood out in the shade of a tree writing her impressions until the last moment. Not far away, Matt took some final photographs.

"Not enough time," Matt said as they climbed onto the bus together.

Her feeling precisely, but she was not even going to answer him. She sat down next to Evan on the front bus seat. How she'd like to return to spend days roaming through these ruins when she wasn't so upset.

Minutes later, the ruins and Uxmal were far behind them.

"Time for lunch," Jacob said as they pulled off the road into a driveway leading through low green jungle to a modern two-story hotel.

In the ladies' lounge at the hotel, Paula combed her hair and was grateful to see that the welt on her lip was receding. Her face was slightly sunburned despite the morning's overcast sky.

Vanessa and her mother stepped into the lounge, and Vanessa asked, "Whatever happened to your lip?"

Paula flushed, but fortunately didn't look any redder in the mirror. "Mosquito bite."

"Really?" Mrs. Perotta said in disbelief.

Let them think what they want, Paula decided, grabbing her shoulder bag and hurrying out to the hotel lobby.

In the new downstairs dining room, she quickly found a table with some elderly members of the Santa Rosita group. "Aren't you married to that blond fellow?" one of the men asked. "I thought I saw him leaving your room this morning."

"No. He and Josh are roommates. He only stopped in to get something." *A kiss!* she thought angrily.

"He's very handsome," one of the women remarked. "And the one you were sitting with on the bus is nice looking too."

"We're old friends," Paula said lightly. If only everyone would leave her alone about Matt and now Evan!

The conversation shifted to their morning at Uxmal, then to the afternoon's excursion to the ruins at Kabah. There was a feeling of camaraderie among them, as if they'd all set out on a great expedition, and Paula began to relax.

For lunch there were refreshing watermelon slices and a delicious cabbage soup. The huipil-clad waitresses and white uniformed busboys moved with a quiet efficiency throughout the large dining room. Outside the tall windows, a beautiful swimming pool was surrounded by coconut palms, hibiscus, and jacaranda trees.

At least she was having a respite from Matt and Evan, Paula thought as she enjoyed the entrée: chicken steamed with onions and peppers, served over rice, and accompanied by a scoop of the thick Mayan black beans. For dessert, their waitress served a delectable custard cake with bright green frosting.

At two o'clock as the bus set out for nearby Kabah, Mayan women walked along the road carrying bright parasols against the sun. "Where are they going?" Paula asked. There had been no villages for miles.

"They live back in the jungle," Jacob explained. "They come here to work at the hotel."

"How on earth do they live in the jungle?" someone inquired.

Jacob shrugged. "As they have in their huts for centuries. There are wild turkeys, deer, and quail for them to eat. They have small garden patches and cornfields, and honey to sell. Their husbands hunt and gather honey."

Beside her Evan remarked, "They look happy."

"Just what I was thinking," she replied.

Within minutes, the driver pulled the bus off alongside the road. As they climbed off, the afternoon's heat and humidity hit. Evan joined Paula as Jacob led them down a well-trodden path into the jungle.

Overhead, the sky had turned bright blue with great puffy white clouds; a buzzard circled over the trees. On the path, a huge iguana slunk lazily toward the underbrush. Beyond, at a turn in the jungle pathway, there was a great corbeled arch that looked like a triumphal entry to a city. There was no building around it, nothing except a crushed white limestone pathway into the tangle of trees and underbrush.

"The *sacbe,* the sacred white road," Jacob explained. "The arch signals the beginning of the path that once carried torchlit Mayan religious processions to Uxmal through the jungle by moonlight. It was also the commercial road upon which slaves carried salt and wood on their backs for trading. These people did not use wheels, nor anything round like the sun which they worshiped—so they carried their goods."

"Fools," Evan said.

Paula ignored him, taking notes.

After a while Matt joined her to take pictures. "Paula, I really am sorry about this morning."

"I don't want to talk about it anymore." She walked away. He would only hurt her again, she told herself over and over as she returned to the bus. There was no point in even discussing it with him.

When they were all aboard the bus again, it was only a minute's drive across the road to the central ruins of Kabah. The driver parked their bus in a parking lot inhabited by eight turkeys.

When they had congregated around Jacob, he said, "The most famous building is straight ahead, the Temple of the Masks. You will see its façade is completely covered by the masks of the long-nosed rain god, Chac."

Paula strolled across the field with the others to the ruins. Indeed the entire facade of the temple was a frieze of Chac masks, row upon eloquent row of projecting snouts mutely beseeching the rain god's favor. Kabah, she recalled from her research, was nearly untouched; archeologists had only renovated the one temple. Other temple tops had fallen down. Yellow butterflies fluttered among the ruins and the encroaching jungle.

Beside her, Matt looked determined to ignore their last interchange, though his voice sounded strained. "I understand that cities like this once connected the entire province every four miles. Wish I could get an overall shot of this, but I doubt that Tom Timmons would spring for a private plane."

She tried to appear preoccupied, making notes about weeds sprouting from the unexcavated mounds—the jungle reclaiming people's work.

It was a short climb up worn limestone steps to the Temple of the Masks, where the frieze and cornices were still in good condition. Unfortunately many of the elephantlike noses of Chac, the rain god, had been stolen by looters and undoubtedly sold.

"The priest would climb down these steps, which were made to look like the back of an alligator," Jacob said, then went on to explain how the Mayan priesthood was passed down to the eldest son.

"Power, always the quest for power," Matt said beside her.

Paula made no comment, but edged slowly away from him. Wasn't that what Matt had done in creating his electronics company? Wasn't his quest for money the same thing? And hadn't he used his physical power on her this morning?

As the group moved through the ruins, the smell of smoke reached them—somewhere a Mayan farmer was burning back the jungle to plant his cornfield.

How primitive it still is, Paula wrote in her notebook. *Yet how surprising after so many centuries to see ruin after ruin still not quite overtaken by the jungle.*

Had it been hacked back by the archeological expeditions or was the clearing the result of the caretakers' efforts? She'd have to ask later.

When they returned to the parking lot, Evan awaited her with a cold soft drink and a seat under a thatch-roofed ramada. It seemed that the caretaker of Kabah—owner of the turkeys bobbing about around them—also ran the concession stand with his smiling wife and children. Just behind the stand was his thatch-roofed house.

Upon their return to the hotel in Merida, Matt asked her, "Don't you think we should have some photos of the marketplace?"

"Yes, and I should see it, I suppose. Just give me a few minutes to freshen up." She felt exhausted.

Ten minutes later, in the lobby, she was pleased to see that others, including Gayle and Josh, would accompany them. Starting out through the city, she noted how different the crowded sidewalks and streets were in comparison with yesterday's light Sunday traffic. University students and office workers, just let out, flooded the streets. On the corners, women vendors sold carved papayas as well as pungent hot sausages roasted with onions.

In the *mercado*, the marketplace, the colorful shops were jammed together and crowded with bustling housewives and workers. At a wicker shop, Gayle and Josh purchased some lidded baskets. "They're for keeping rolls warm at the table," Gayle said.

"Ah, domesticity!" Matt teased them.

Paula bought two of the baskets for herself.

When they returned to the hotel at seven o'clock, Paula told Gayle, "I'm so tired, I have to go to bed."

"I hope you're not getting sick," Gayle fretted.

"I'll be fine tomorrow."

"You'll miss dinner and the nightclub show here in the hotel."

"I'm afraid I don't even care," she admitted as she undressed. She slipped into her blue nightgown and lay down on the bed. "I'd appreciate your making mental notes of the evening for me."

"Of course, I will."

She'd been dreaming something dreadful when Gayle returned from dinner and the show hours later. "Was it good?" Paula asked groggily.

"Not as good as last night. Pretty much the same dances."

"What about Matt?"

"He was with Vanessa."

Paula rolled over, numbed with exhaustion. When she finally fell asleep again, the dreadful dream continued, ending with Matt and Vanessa in a passionate embrace.

chapter

7

SHE SAT ON THE EDGE of her bed and sleepily watched Gayle trundle her suitcase into the hotel hallway.

"Are you sure that you don't want me to call the hotel doctor?" Gayle asked. "You look dreadfully pale."

"I'll be fine," Paula replied, forcing herself to stand up. She'd have to pack and get dressed, she reminded herself, though her mind seemed so fuzzy that nothing came into focus. She would *have* to be fine! This afternoon they'd visit the gem of the Yucatan's archeological ruins—Chichen Itza.

Gayle looked uncertain about departing. "Are you positive that you'll be all right?"

"I'm certain," Paula insisted, though she felt far from it. A headache lurked behind her eyes, and she was dizzy.

Gayle sighed in resignation. "Don't forget to leave your suitcase out in the hallway by seven-thirty."

Paula smiled wanly. "This morning you *are* playing mother hen. I've already called room service. All I need is some coffee, and I'll come around."

"I hope so," Gayle said as she closed the door behind her.

At length, the same bellboy who'd delivered yesterday's breakfast arrived with her tray—and this time there was no Matt.

The steaming hot coffee revived her, scrambled eggs and toast satisfied her hunger, and an aspirin masked her headache. In the mirror, her sapphire blue cotton blouse and crisp white bermuda shorts did wonders for her appearance. Fortunately, the Yucatan's humidity enhanced the natural waves of her blond hair.

By the time she stepped outside the hotel to catch the tour bus, she felt slightly better. She stopped to buy one of the inexpensive Meridan straw hats for the day's outing. As she waited for the vendor to make change, she noticed that Matt and Vanessa were shopping across the street. No doubt they were now "an item," and she'd been saved from further romantic agonies.

Moments later as Matt crossed the street toward her, his eye contact was quick and volcanic. She stood transfixed.

"How are you, Paula?" he inquired. "Gayle said you're not feeling well."

"I'm fine, thank you," she replied evenly. She accepted her change from the hat vendor, and when she turned, Matt was still gazing at her.

Vanessa slipped her arm through his. "Let's get a good seat. Paula and *her friend,* Evan, had the front one yesterday." She turned him away with a proprietary hand on his arm.

Paula crammed the straw hat on her head.

Evan stepped to her side. "I missed you last night," he said with a warm glow in his brown eyes. "I hope you're feeling better."

"Yes, thanks." She glanced thoughtfully at him. How kind he was. She'd never really known him in high school, not from three or four dates. She added, "I slept and slept and slept."

"You still look sleepy. You're certain you weren't up doing all of the nightspots?" he teased.

Paula laughed. "That would have been the last thing I needed."

He smiled, but his eyes probed hers seriously through his horn-rimmed glasses. For an instant Paula suspected he didn't believe her, but that was foolish. "We'd better get on the bus," she suggested and headed for it.

Vanessa had indeed wangled the front seat with Matt this morning. "It's a good seat for taking pictures," he said as Paula climbed on.

"Yes, it is," she agreed coolly and started down the aisle.

The only seats left were in the very back of the bus. She and Evan settled by the window in the shade, yet by the time they left Merida, their window was directly in the sun's glare.

Jacob discussed the passing sights, and Paula took notes, becoming increasingly drowsy as they rode through the countryside. *Windmills whirl over unkempt sisal fields by abandoned haciendas,* she wrote. *Cajonal—the yellow wild-flowers from which bees make honey for local consumption and export. Brahma cattle . . . a sisal shredding plant . . . villages with their clusters of oval huts surrounded by garden patches and banana, orange, and papaya trees . . . an abandoned church with no roof . . .*

She dozed off, and her head bumped against the window. Awakening, she glanced out sleepily and wrote again. *A small boy carrying a bucket of shelled corn to be ground . . . a woman cooking over an outdoor fire . . .*

Her mind wandered, and her eyes drifted shut again. After a while she remembered Matt holding her in the horse-drawn calesa, and she leaned against him contentedly. How wonderful to nestle on his shoulder and chest. The ride seemed endless, but she lay serenely in his arms.

"Paula . . . ?" Evan said softly. "Time to wake up."

She opened her eyes with a start. She'd been sleeping on

Evan's shoulder, his arm around her! "I'm sorry!" she blurted, sitting up.

"My pleasure," he murmured, and rubbed his arm.

"Your arm must have gone to sleep. . . ."

He smiled. "Any time you want someone to cuddle up to, I'm available."

She blushed. "How long did I sleep?"

"Over an hour."

A new problem occurred to her. "I didn't take notes!"

"What a determined reporter you are," Evan said with a chuckle. "But there's no need to worry; I watched everything for you. Nothing much new—villages, abandoned sisal fields, and low jungle."

"Thanks!" It was bad enough to have missed everything for notetaking, but she'd wanted to enjoy every moment of the trip. She glanced out the window at a Mayan village as the bus parked in front of a modern two-story hotel. "Where are we?"

"Piste. We're going to get settled, then eat lunch before we journey out to Chichen Itza."

"Well, I'm not going to sleep through Chichen Itza!" she said, savoring the sound of the exotic name on her tongue. She would enjoy Chichen Itza and the rest of the trip *despite* Matt and Vanessa, despite anything, she decided as she gathered up her carry-on case, straw hat, handbag, and notebook.

Evan said, "You look much better now."

"How did I look before?" she asked in a wry tone.

"Pretty tired. Pretty and tired, that is."

"Now, Evan!" she protested.

Stepping out of the bus, Paula followed the group through tropical plantings to the hotel's outdoor registration desk near the pool. Joining the line, she discovered Vanessa's mother in front of her. Since they'd scarcely spoken to each other on the trip, she asked, "Are you having a good time, Mrs. Perotta?"

The woman simply cast a chilly look at her.

Vanessa and Matt, standing in the next line, witnessed the encounter. Matt's lips drew back in a hard line. "Did you sleep well on the bus, Paula?" he asked.

"Yes, as a matter of fact I did." How had he noticed from the front seat? Had he come all the way to the back of the bus to see her? "I've been terribly tired. I dozed off."

"So I noticed."

He had come to see her!

Behind her Evan explained, "I didn't think I should wake you. At any rate, Matt said it wasn't important—just an idea for the articles."

Paula looked aside as tears misted her eyes. She was aware of Gayle standing to the side of the group, shepherding them along and probably seeing the entire scene too.

Mrs. Perotta stepped forward to the registration clerk. "I want a single room tonight, and I don't mind paying for it." She glanced at Vanessa and Matt in the adjoining line. "I've never been known to stand in the way of romance."

Appalled, Paula bit her trembling lower lip as she listened to the clerk make the arrangements. What kind of mother would encourage her daughter like that? The idea of it was repugnant, absolutely horrid. If that was the sort of person Matt wanted to associate with, Paula thought, then she shouldn't even want to have anything to do with him!

Her emotions in chaos, she stepped to the registration desk. At the adjacent clerk's counter area, Matt and Vanessa obtained their keys—to adjoining rooms no doubt!

Once her arrangements were made, Paula grabbed her key and rushed up the outdoor stairway to her second-floor room. As she rounded the turn in the stairwell, she glimpsed Matt

127

and Vanessa heading up the opposite stairway to the other wing of the building.

By the time she let herself into her room, her jaw was stiff with anger, her teeth clenched. She closed the door behind her, scarcely aware of the room as she stared uncomprehendingly into space.

Moments later, Gayle unlocked the door and stepped in, turning a concerned look on Paula. "Lovely room, isn't it?" she asked uneasily. "I didn't know what to expect here."

Paula looked around, seeing the room in a daze: glossy red tile floors, white walls, dark carved furniture, heavy draperies with geometric designs. Outside the sliding glass door, a wrought-iron railing enclosed the balcony overlooking the Mayan village of Piste. "It's fine," she said, sitting down dully on one of the twin beds.

"Are you going to have lunch?" Gayle asked in a careful voice. She turned to the mirror to tidy her upswept red curls with her fingertips, though her eyes were on Paula.

Paula shook her head. How could she possibly enter the dining room? By now it was obvious to everyone in the group that Matt had thrown her over for Vanessa.

"You have to eat," Gayle said.

Paula's heart twisted with anguish. Without warning, a sob escaped from the depths of her soul. She buried her face in the bedspread, weeping uncontrollably. How could this happen to her again? Why couldn't she find someone wonderful and dependable who would love her in return? Why did the men she fell in love with have to be Matts and Tonys?

She felt Gayle's hand rubbing her back. "Just get it out," she said softly. "Let all of your hurt out so you don't bury it and get all hard inside. Just cry it all out."

Much to her chagrin, Paula sobbed all the harder. She was barely aware of the door opening and of the embarrassed Mayan maid backing out with an armful of towels.

"Crying is supposed to be good for you," Gayle said, "but it certainly doesn't seem like it at the time."

Paula sobbed, "Why does this happen to me? Why can't I find someone like Josh who will love me and not hurt me?"

"I don't know," Gayle answered, her green eyes awash with compassion. "I'd so like to help you." She gave Paula a handful of folded tissues from her purse.

Paula blew her nose and wiped away her tears.

"The truth is that I think only God can help you," Gayle said seriously.

What did God have to do with this? As far as she could see, *if* he existed, he was allowing this to happen to her. Maybe he really was way out there in the universe ... occasionally looking down on people as if they were ants scurrying in all directions. She'd never understand Gayle's kind of faith.

"Would you let me pray for you?" Gayle asked.

Paula lifted her shoulders dejectedly. "If you really think it would do any good. . . ."

Gayle reached for her hands.

"You mean now?" Paula protested, backing away. Her fingertips felt icy in Gayle's warm hands.

"Why not now?" Gayle responded, holding her hands firmly. She closed her eyes.

It appeared as if there were nothing else to do, and Paula reluctantly closed her eyes too.

"Heavenly Father," Gayle began, "we come to you with our hearts full of thanksgiving over this matter of Matt and Vanessa seemingly involved with each other."

Seemingly involved? Paula chafed. As for *hearts full of thanksgiving*—she felt no thankfulness at all.

Gayle continued, "We thank you and trust you, even though we don't always understand what is happening. We know that you never send trouble, and you want us to give thanks in absolutely everything."

It sounded absurd. Paula fretted, not finding an ounce of thanksgiving in her heart.

"We praise you, Heavenly Father," Gayle said with a voice full of trust. "We know what mighty works you can do, but so often we forget that it's so very simple for you to provide for our smaller earthly concerns too."

Smaller earthly concerns! Paula railed.

"We ask now a special blessing on Paula, that she might find your wisdom and guidance in this entire matter," Gayle prayed. "We ask in the name of our Savior, Jesus, and thank you, Father. Amen."

Gayle squeezed her hands for an instant, then moved away. "And now let's clean up and sit by the pool until it's time for lunch."

"I can't," Paula protested.

"You can," Gayle said firmly. "You can and you will. You have nothing in the world to be ashamed of."

"Stupidity," Paula replied.

"Let's count our blessings," Gayle said, trying to cheer her.

At the moment, Paula couldn't think of a single one.

After they had cleaned up, Paula donned her dark glasses, determined to hide the ravages of her grief. As they walked downstairs, there were still twenty minutes before lunchtime.

Josh waited patiently on a poolside chaise lounge for Gayle. "The gift shop looks interesting," he said.

"Marvelous," Gayle replied. "That's just what we women need, a good bout of shopping."

Paula mustered a wan smile, grateful Gayle had included her when she and Josh might prefer to be alone. Gayle was a true friend. That, at least, was a blessing.

In the quiet gift shop Paula eased away to avoid intruding upon them. After a while her despair lifted slightly, and she found a light, delicately woven white stole at such a reasonable price that she bought one for herself, another to set aside as a gift. Besides the ever-present white embroidered huipils, guayabera shirts, and hand-painted pottery, there were unique Mayan temple rubbings, colorful yarn dolls of Mayan dancers, and numerous handmade items

She looked up and Evan was at her side. "Where did you come from?"

"I saw you across the pool. I was hoping that you'd join me for lunch."

Why not? Lunching with him would be better than walking into the hotel dining room alone—or tagging along with Gayle and Josh. "Thanks," she said. "I'd like to." She'd only have to be careful not to encourage him.

Later in the vast white dining room, no one mentioned her dark glasses. No one except Gayle—and maybe Evan and Josh—cared anyhow.

In the buffet line, she helped herself to a light lunch: cabbage slaw, a cucumber salad, carrot sticks, slices of turkey, and a huge chunk of papaya for dessert. As she and Evan wound their way to a table by the window, she glimpsed Matt, Vanessa, and Mrs. Perotta entering the room.

"Steady," Evan counseled from behind her.

Was her upset that obvious? she fretted, then realized Evan had warned her to steady her tilting salad plate.

When they were seated, a waitress stopped by to offer cola or coffee. The woman peered momentarily at Paula. It was the maid who'd walked into the room with towels during her tears.

"Something wrong?" Evan asked solicitously.

"Nothing," Paula responded with a shake of her head.

After a while he asked, "Aren't you going to eat?"

She promptly picked at her chilled salads, papaya, and turkey.

131

After lunch she and Evan rested in poolside chaises until it was time to board the bus. She didn't even want to speculate where Matt might be with Vanessa. In any event, he was absolutely not going to spoil her outing at Chichen Itza!

At boarding time, Jacob waited beside the bus as the group climbed on. "And now Chichen Itza, the jewel of the Yucatan."

Paula found herself saying, "I hope so, after so many years of hearing about it."

"I guarantee that you won't be disappointed," Jacob stated. "If you have any special questions, be sure to ask. Your photographer said that you're writing articles for a newspaper."

"Yes," Paula responded, wondering how Matt happened to tell Jacob that.

She passed Matt without a glance. He was apparently saving a window seat for Vanessa.

"Here's a good place," Evan suggested, and Paula sat down with him in the middle of the bus.

Finally everyone was seated, Vanessa last as expected, wearing a strapless black sundress that showed off far more than her tan.

Paula looked out the window as the bus took off. The actual village of Piste appeared to be back beyond the main road. Judging by the construction of hotels, gas stations, and restaurants, the main highway was turning into a commercial zone. Sad. "I'd like to explore the village," she thought aloud.

"Tonight," Evan answered. "We can take it in tonight."

It seemed only minutes later that the scenery changed from village to low jungle, and before long they pulled into a chalky white parking lot jammed with other tour buses.

"Chichen Itza!" Jacob announced.

Outside, the air was hot and humid, but their group gathered excitedly under the shade of a huge Indian laurel tree. Jacob said, "We begin at New Chichen, which is sometimes called Kukulcan—Mayan for the Quetzalcoatl of the Toltecs, who arrived as a god and a myth in the tenth century when the warlike Toltecs invaded. However, the real Kukulcan did not arrive until the middle of the thirteenth century. . . ."

Paula was surprised to find Matt at her side, his camera ready.

"What's the slant for this article?" he asked in a businesslike tone.

"I don't have a specific slant yet. It will be on Chichen Itza and the surrounding area."

"Fine," he responded equably.

"Let's go," Jacob said and the group moved eagerly along behind him to the entry gate.

Paula glanced at Vanessa. She did not look pleased about Matt's working with Paula. Evan, regretfully, didn't look too thrilled either at the moment.

Passing through the crowded entry gate into New Chichen Itza, Paula was struck by the incongruous expanse of manicured grass stretching out in all directions, then by the awesome hulk of a grayish pyramid looming skyward before her. "El Castillo?" she asked.

"El Castillo," Jacob replied. "So named because the Spanish thought it a fortress—castle. But for the Mayans, this was a temple for sun worship. You see the four massive stairways facing the cardinal points, each with 91 steps, adding up to 364—plus one, the summit—totaling 365, the number of days in a year."

Paula took rapid notes as he continued.

". . . 52 panels on the sides, corresponding to the number

133

of years in the Toltec religious calendar . . . 18 sections of terraces on each side, representing their eighteen-month year. The pyramid was built over earlier construction, probably dating from the early time of Toltec occupation.

"Now, for our climbers, there is a wonderfully preserved Chac Mool—you remember the reclining figure with the sacrificial plate on his abdomen—and a jade-inlaid jaguar throne of the priest inside. . . ."

Matt darted a questioning glance at her. "You going to climb again?"

"Why not?" she replied. This time they'd at least be going up the pyramid inside El Castillo. It was unlike the pyramid at Uxmal that was a platform out in the sky.

Jacob waved them on. "Okay, climbers!"

Paula looked up at the towering pyramid and caught a deep breath.

"You're not going up again?" Evan asked.

She nodded determinedly.

Making her way to the pyramid's entry in silence with Matt, she thought she at least might try to mend their old friendship. "Look at that sky," she began. "You were saying at Uxmal that you preferred a blue sky with white clouds. Now you have it, though they do have gray linings."

He glanced at the sky. "Yes, a very dramatic sky—sunny, yet tropical. Looks as if a storm lurks in every one of those clouds."

Like her own confused emotions lately, she mused.

Vanessa, not intending to climb El Castillo, stood aside with her mother as Matt and Paula joined fellow climbers near a small entry at the base of the pyramid's north stairway.

They'd barely begun making their way up the damp, narrow passageway when the entire line of people stopped abruptly. Matt bumped into her. Her knees went weak, and she caught her breath.

"Sorry," he apologized.

She didn't answer. Would she never overcome her attraction to him?

Gasping tourists pressed past her on their way down the dimly lit stone stairwell.

"Is the climb worth it?" someone in the line of climbers behind her asked.

"It's dark, hot, and exhausting. We gave up."

Matt asked, "Paula, are you sure you want to do this?"

"You couldn't pay me to quit," she insisted, as much to assure herself as him.

Later, after ascending the steep slippery steps steadily for a long time, there was still no end in sight. Her legs ached and her white T-shirt and bermudas felt drenched with perspiration, yet she was determined not to quit.

The middle-aged threesome in front of her turned back. "We just can't make it," they admitted miserably.

When Paula decided she couldn't manage another step, someone said, "Almost there."

Twenty steps later, the stone monolith of Chac Mool loomed in front of her, his plate ready for a sacrifice. Her heart pounded so hard that it might have been a live heart delivered to him.

"Shall I take your picture sitting on the sacrificial plate?" Matt joked breathlessly.

"If I sit down," she gasped, "I'll never stand up again."

She mounted the final steps to the poorly lit throne room and stood behind the protective grill. The red jaguar throne! From this primitive bench Mayan priests had ruled Chichen Itza for centuries. Although encrusted with chunks of jade, there was nothing elegant about it. "It looks barbarous," she decided with a shudder as Matt stepped beside her to take pictures. "Primitive and barbaric."

"It was a bloodthirsty religion," Matt remarked.

Someone behind them in the stairwell said, "Aren't they all?"

"One bad religion is no reason to condemn them all," Matt answered with a hint of passion in his voice.

Paula cast a sidelong glance at him, then turned again to the throne room. Her mind flashed back to the time when he was a teenager speaking so eloquently in church. Surely he'd outgrown that during his quest for power and money.

She turned her attention to the musty throne room, making mental notes for her article about the damp prisonlike cell. Beside her, Matt snapped picture after picture, varying the speed and aperture to compensate for the darkness since flash bulbs were not allowed.

Seconds later, it was time to leave.

"Let me go ahead of you," Matt insisted, starting down the steep steps first. "I remember the look on your face coming down the pyramid at Uxmal."

"I'm fine," she insisted, though she wished for a handrail. The rock walls of the pyramid were wet from constant humidity and lack of sun and air. Climbing down, the steps seemed steeper than before.

She squinted through the murky light, barely seeing the steps, feeling with each foot. Descending was far worse than climbing up. Climbers ascending the steps in the narrow passageway stopped to let her and Matt pass. She noticed that he made his way down slowly, occasionally turning to wait for her.

"You all right?" he asked.

"Fine, thanks—"

Suddenly her foot slid over a slippery step. Jerking her arms up for balance, she plunged forward in the near darkness, a short scream ripping from her throat.

"Paula!" Matt cried out. He reached up and grabbed her in his arms, staggering, then braced himself against the wet wall.

She clung to him, eyes closed in relief and pressing her face into his shoulder. "I'm sorry," she finally apologized, still trembling. "I nearly took you down with me!"

"I owed you one," he answered.

She pulled away. "What do you mean?"

"Don't you remember when you caught me falling off the kitchen stool at home?"

"You remember that?"

"How could I not remember falling into the arms of a beautiful woman?"

She didn't answer. She presumed he recalled her bringing him the roses then too.

He turned to move on. "Ready?"

"Yes." His recollection so surprised her that she descended the rest of the ancient steps far more quickly.

The Santa Rosita group waited near the base of El Castillo. "You look absolutely white," Gayle said to Paula. "What happened?"

Paula answered, "Nothing much."

"She almost fell," Matt said.

"You'd better sit down," Evan suggested, taking her arm.

"No, I just need to catch my breath for a minute," she insisted. She wasn't certain what had shaken her most: the momentary plunge into the darkness, Matt's catching her in his arms and holding her so firmly, or his remembering the day of the roses.

When they strolled to the ancient ballcourt near El Castillo, Matt rushed ahead to take pictures while Paula made notes. The two stone rings used as ball hoops still protruded from the walls. Jacob explained, "The players could only hit the rubber ball with forearms, hips and buttocks, which were

137

covered with pads. The game was deadly serious—so serious that the losers were often sacrificed."

Matt eyed the Temple of the Jaguars built into a side of the ballcourt. "How shall we do this shot?"

"Lots of close-ups of the jaguars on the frieze, I think. And some good distant shots too."

Later Evan accompanied her along the Mayan's *sache*. The broad sacred road led through the jungle to Chichen Itza's famous *cenote*—the Well of Sacrifices. The dark foreboding waters of the well were surrounded by sheer rock walls.

At the upper rim were the remains of a small temple that Jacob explained had probably been used as a steambath for purification rites. "The well was believed to be the home of the rain god, Chac," Jacob said. "It was used only for ritualistic purposes. During droughts or other disasters, children—drugged with copal to calm their struggling—were thrown into the water to plead for help from Chac. Their bones as well as gold and jade have been dredged out."

Paula shuddered.

"I thought they only threw in virgins," Evan commented.

"Children under twelve, according to the archeologists," Jacob answered.

Paula glanced at Evan, speculating on his view of virginity. She suspected that it would be more important to him than to someone as experienced as Matt.

Looking away, she found Matt and Vanessa watching them. It occurred to Paula that complications like hers had happened throughout the centuries—that her anguish over Matt was nothing new or unusual. Surely it had happened to Mayan maidens, different as their culture had been. The old phrase was "eternal triangle." Eternal indeed!

When they left New Chichen Itza and crossed the road to enter the original Mayan settlement, Matt took pictures of a darling barefoot Mayan girl in her white huipil. Perhaps three or four years old, she posed with delight and pointed out her thatch-roofed house in the caretakers' village. Bright clothing flapped from lines strung among the banana trees, a pig lay in the shade, and turkeys bobbed through the grass, much as they might have centuries ago.

Matt seemed quite taken with the child. "Ask her if she speaks Spanish," Matt suggested to Paula.

Paula questioned her, but the girl replied in a Mayan dialect. "I read that some Mayans refuse to speak anything except their native tongue," she explained.

The tiny girl trailed happily along with them, smiling at their wonder over the ruins of her forefathers in Old Chichen Itza, especially the amazing ancient observatory.

"El Caracol, the snail," Jacob translated. "Mayan astronomers charted the heavens from it as early as the fifth century. Using its data, priests selected auspicious days for planting and harvesting, warning the people of eclipses and the need for sacrifices."

"It seems as if we've really entered another century," Paula said as Matt took pictures from all angles. There were very few other tourists in Old Chichen and almost no restoration of the ruins. When they climbed to the top of a small pyramid, it appeared that the dark green jungle could swallow all of the ruins in a matter of days.

Paula noticed Matt posing the Mayan girl in front of the various ruins as they left. The pictures would be spectacular for this article.

The girl followed behind them, now carrying a long sprig of wild lilac she'd picked up somewhere at the edge of the jungle. At the bus, Matt offered her money for posing for the pictures, but she shook her head. Instead, she pulled down his face to hers, ran her fingers through his golden hair, then kissed his cheek.

"Really, Matt, isn't she a bit young?" Vanessa asked, and his color rose, though it didn't seem to spoil his pleasure.

The child, her brown eyes shining, handed Paula the sprig of wild lilac and danced away. Standing outside the bus, she waved at them as they settled into their seats: Paula with Evan, Matt with Vanessa.

When the bus pulled out of the parking lot, Paula returned the girl's waves, then inhaled deeply of the fragrant wild lilac. Why had the girl wanted to kiss Matt? Was it his blond hair? It would be unusual for the dark Mayans, but surely there were many other blond tourists. Or was it something she sensed about him? Possibly the same attributes that she herself had been attracted to years ago?

She decided to press the sprig of flowers in her guidebook, not only for its beauty, but to remember the lovely Mayan child who had kissed Matt so tenderly . . . and given the flowers to her. The gesture struck her as what Gayle would call a blessing.

chapter

8

WHEN THEY RETURNED TO THE HOTEL in Piste, Paula felt hot, exhausted, and covered with dust. Hurrying upstairs to her room for a shower, she caught a glimpse of the men below. Matt stood near the pool talking with Josh and Evan. It struck her as curious that Evan would be included in the conversation, though she supposed they were merely discussing the day's events.

Later, as she returned downstairs refreshed, she found only Evan waiting on a poolside lounge. He stood immediately, looking neat in a clean white polo shirt and tan slacks. "Ready to check out the village?" he asked.

"Ready!" she replied. Her yellow notebook was now smudged and creased, but, as always, in hand. "Good. You're carrying your camera."

"Thought I'd try some shots for your articles," he explained.

There was no point encouraging unreal expectations. "The *Times* is paying very little, and the pictures will be chosen by the editor."

"Don't worry, I just thought it'd be fun to have some pictures published," he responded and propelled her by the arm toward the hotel entrance. "Matt doesn't have a contract with them, does he?"

"No, not at all. But he used to do a lot of photography for the *Times* when he was in high school."

Evan shrugged. "Matt used to do *everything* when he was in high school."

Jealousy? That seemed absurd. Matt was five years older and had been in college when Evan entered Santa Rosita High. Still, Matt had made quite a mark in the community as a young leader. She supposed that mothers asked their sons, "Why can't you be more like Matt Montgomery?" His business success very likely galled many young Santa Rosita men too.

As she and Evan walked alongside the highway, occasional trucks roared by, heading for Cancun. Mayan men arrived home in Piste for the evening in crowded pickup trucks; others rode bicycles, some with bundles of firewood strapped to the rear racks. Beautiful brown children ran out to greet them.

"Do you want to look at the shops?" Evan asked, nodding toward the colorful tourist attractions across the street.

She calculated about an hour of good light remained for pictures. "I'd rather walk into the village as long as we're not too intrusive. Maybe we could stop at the shops when it gets dark."

Behind the roadside restaurants, hotels, bars, and shops, they found a dirt road leading into the residential area of the village. Trees with heavy clusters of bananas hung over the rock walls and acacia pole fences; the oval thatch-roofed huts were interspersed with brightly painted modern stucco dwellings. Open doors and windows welcomed the slightest breezes, and, inside, the natives rested in hammocks slung from the ceilings.

"Don't they have beds?" Evan asked.

Paula shook her head. "Not according to what I've read.

Mattresses would probably be covered with mildew within days after rainy season begins!"

Three little Mayan girls joined them, whispering and giggling as they skipped along, reminding Paula of the child at Chichen Itza, but these requested money to pose for Evan's pictures. He didn't seem to mind. As they moved through the village, he took photos of bright red flowers amid the tropical greenery, a white steer gazing at them through an acacia pole corral, a small park with its statue of a mother and baby, and a church playground where boys played soccer and teenage girls sat on benches to applaud.

Paula approached one of the schoolgirls. "Is this your church?" she asked in Spanish.

"Iglesia vieja," the girl answered. The old church. She pointed out the modernistic church on the other side of the playground as if expecting it to be of more interest.

"May we take pictures of the old church?" Paula asked.

"Sí," the girl responded with a flash of pride, although the old church had obviously fallen into neglect and now appeared abandoned.

Paula walked up the worn wooden steps of the church. She and Evan halted at the sight of people and household furnishings inside the open door. An elderly woman sitting on a couch waved them in. "Would you like to see the church?" she asked with a Mayan lilt to her Spanish.

"Sí," Paula replied.

"Maybe we shouldn't," Evan said, hanging back. "They *live* in here!"

The smiling woman motioned insistently that they enter. Apparently visitors were truly welcome.

As Paula and Evan stepped in, the woman led them through the living quarters to a simple but charming yellow sanctuary, then made her departure.

Paula's eyes went to the slightly raised altar, where a hand-hewn wooden table served as a pulpit. Behind it, arched niches held fresh flowers and endearing figures of Jesus. Fans suspended from the ceiling hung motionless, and perhaps twenty rustic wooden benches awaited a congregation.

Sitting down on a worn pew, a feeling of peace crept through her. She was aware of Evan's camera clicking, then of his leaving by the side door, but a sense of holiness held her in place. It was as if the prayers of the parishioners still lingered, filling the sanctuary with faith. She recalled that she had just returned from Chichen Itza, one of the most religious sites of the Mayan civilization, without feeling a trace of love or even a closeness to God. Here in the simple old church, a gentle love filled the sanctuary, blessing it so that she was compelled to bow in prayer.

For an instant she had no idea of what to say, then finally the words came. *Heavenly Father,* she prayed, *if you're real, if Jesus is real—I would so like to know. I suppose it seems terribly presumptuous of me, but I truly want to understand.* She could think of nothing else except something she had learned in Sunday school as a child. *I pray in the name of Jesus. Amen.*

She opened her eyes and sat for a long time, wondering if somehow she might receive an answer, but there was nothing except the look of love in the eyes of the figure of Jesus. Reluctantly she stood up and walked through the pews to the side door.

Outside, Evan waited, raising an eyebrow at her. "I didn't know you were religious," he said.

"I don't know that I am," she replied. Her years of Sunday school didn't seem to take, though occasionally she thought to say The Lord's Prayer at bedtime. That was the extent of her spiritual life. She assumed from Evan's tone of voice and previous comments that he wasn't "religious"—whatever that meant. Suddenly, she felt sad.

On the way back to the hotel, Evan reached for her hand, and she quickly occupied it by jotting notes about the village: *picturesque but slowly departing from the primitive simplicity and charm . . . unfortunately becoming "civilized."* Feeling guilty she said, "I've enjoyed walking through this village nearly as much as I did Merida."

"I just plain enjoy being with you," he replied.

Disconcerted by the warmth in his brown eyes, she finally managed a smile. "Thanks, Evan." She glanced away at her watch. "I guess there is time for shopping before dinner."

At the dinner table in the dining room, she realized that many of their group were missing. "Where are Gayle and Josh?" she asked an elderly couple, part of the Santa Rosita crowd. Matt and Vanessa were absent too, though Mrs. Perotta was at the next table talking with one of the unattached men her age.

The woman beside her looked surprised. "Why, they took taxis to the light and sound show in Chichen Itza. I suppose they're having dinner at one of the hotels there. I thought all of you young people would be going."

"No one asked me," Paula replied, astounded. And she was the one who was supposed to be writing travel articles! She turned to Evan. "Did you know?"

"I did know they were going," he admitted, sipping his wine. "Didn't Gayle ask you?"

Paula shook her head in disappointment. "I can't imagine. . . ."

After dinner she was still annoyed at not being invited to the light and sound show in Chichen Itza. Strolling on the hotel's garden paths with Evan, she tried to forget her irritation. The sultry tropical air had cooled slightly, and her spirits lifted at seeing the night sky filled with stars. Moonlight illumined the crushed limestone under their feet, reminding her of the ancient Mayans' white paths for religious processions. Soft night sounds from the nearby jungle lent an exotic atmosphere to the evening.

They sat down on the chaises by the pool, but after a short while she said, "I think I'd better turn in. I can't imagine why I've been so tired."

"It's the humidity. We're just not used to it in California," Evan suggested.

She shrugged. "Probably. I'll see you in the morning."

"I'll walk you to the door, Paula."

"It's not necessary." After what she'd gone through with Matt, she did not want to get involved with any more romantic good-night scenes.

"I'll feel a lot better about it if I see you safely there," he protested.

"If you really insist . . ." Why was it that she always worried about hurting other people's feelings? she asked herself angrily.

Walking up the stairway, they discussed the next morning's ride to Cancun.

"I'm more interested in that than I was in seeing the ruins," Evan admitted. "You know the Mexican government selected the site for Cancun by computer. They input the climate, rainfall, location, and distance to the ruins—and who knows what else—then the computer chose Cancun as the best possible site in Mexico."

Not wanting to tell him that she'd already researched Cancun's resort beginnings, she quipped, "You're a computer nut!"

Evan grinned, capturing her hand in his. When she looked at him, she was certain that the glints of interest in his eyes had nothing to do with computers.

146

At her door, she quickly inserted the key and turned it. "Thanks, Evan. Good night—"

Before she could rush into the room, he'd caught her by the shoulders and turned her to him.

"Please, no, Evan!" she protested.

He looked hurt as he moved away. "Don't you like me?"

She recalled his disastrous marriage and didn't want to further damage his ego. "Of course I do! Liking you has nothing to do with it! It's just that—that I'm so terribly tired."

"I'll see you in the morning," he said curtly and strode away.

The next morning as Paula hurried out to the hotel parking lot, most of the Santa Rosita group waited in the shade near the bus. Evan stood slightly apart from Gayle, Josh, and Matt, obviously watching for her. "I was about to go upstairs to pull you out of bed," he teased in an intimate tone.

A flood of heat rushed to Paula's cheeks. What on earth did Matt—and Gayle and Josh—think? Surely they realized that Evan was merely trying to be humorous!

Later, when she climbed on the bus, Matt was already sitting with Vanessa, so preoccupied with their conversation that they seemed unaware of her. Paula's spirits drooped as she sat down beside Evan. She opened her notebook. Cancun was about two hours away, and she hadn't taken any notes while sleeping on yesterday's trip. She couldn't afford to skip notes about the countryside today. At least that would keep her mind from Matt!

As the miles passed by, she kept her attention on the passing scenery. She was struck again by the beauty of the small villages with their rock walls. Purple bougainvillaea cascaded over walls and corrals, and red cannas bloomed at

147

the doorway of many of the Mayan houses. The villages were primitive but natural; for once man had almost improved upon nature.

At Vallidad—the last city taken from the Mayans by the Spaniards—pink flowering trees gave a dreamlike quality to the community. "Spanish-speaking people are not welcome in the city," Jacob said. "Many tribes of Mayans—some 2,000 to 3,000 years old— are here, and they do not wish to change their ways. Some of them refuse to have their children learn Spanish in school."

"Sounds like an integration problem," Paula ventured. She noticed a Mexican military installation with uniformed soldiers in plain view.

"And not the kind we'd hear about in our newspapers!" Evan said with vehemence. "Seems to me that all we read about is what's bad about the United States while other countries' problems are overlooked by our reporters. I get mighty sick of it!"

He harbored a lot of suppressed anger, she thought again.

She turned to the window, writing notes as they drove out into the countryside. Mayan men cut the grasses at the roadside with gleaming machetes, and occasionally there were remnants of small cornfields.

"A vulture," Evan said. Leaning close to her, he pointed out the big dark bird circling over a field of bony white cattle. Evan's body brushed against hers and their eyes met.

She quickly looked out the window again, quietly watching the countryside, then finally the construction-choked streets of downtown Cancun. Evan cared for her, and she only wanted to be—What did she want? She'd been so foolish about Matt. Perhaps she was being stupid again, not giving Evan a chance.

She felt a sense of exhilaration as they drove through the

parklike entrance to Cancun's island causeway. The change of scenery was stunning. The Gulf of Mexico shimmered like liquid sapphire to the north; to the south, shadings of turquoise from the Caribbean Sea streaked the blue water.

Ahead, the L-shaped island of Cancun jutted out into the water with its strip of luxury hotels, restaurants, night clubs, discos, tennis courts, and golf courses. Although most of the palm trees were still small, a few already towered in the sky from the long narrow island; yachts and excursion boats plied the waters. Here and there, tourists water-skied, and in the distance, a brave one para-sailed over the sea.

Jacob pointed out the blocks of shops and restaurants. "And there's the international convention center where Ballet Folklorico performances are often featured."

Evan remarked, "I'd like to take you out to dinner there tonight."

"Thank you, Evan. . . ." Something stopped her. "Let's wait first to see how the schedule works out." She glanced toward the front of the bus and saw Matt's blond hair just above the seat.

Jacob said, "There, toward the end of the island, you see El Hotel Pyramide, your hotel."

Paula gave a short laugh. "What would the ancient Mayans say to see their architecture copied by modern hotel chains?"

Minutes later under the hotel's porte-cochere, the disembarking passengers bid their bus driver farewell. Jacob led them to the long registration desk in the cavernous white hotel lobby. "I'll be leaving you now," he said with a touch of regret. He made his individual farewells to everyone in the Santa Rosita group, collecting tips and cordially inviting them all to return to Mexico.

He told Paula with his usual sleepy grin, "Be sure to put me in your articles."

"Of course," she replied facetiously. But he'd no more than left when inspiration hit.

"You're looking very pleased with yourself, Paula," Matt said.

"I've had a brainstorm for the articles—I'm going to use a fictitious tour guide as a mouthpiece!" She explained her idea. "What do you think?"

Matt nodded thoughtfully. "A brilliant way to compress information."

"Some of which might be dull," she put in.

"You really do enjoy writing, don't you?" he asked. "You glow when you talk about it."

"Do I?" she marveled. "All I know is that I especially enjoy it when inspiration hits."

Vanessa, standing at Matt's side, looked annoyed with their conversation.

"Paula does have a degree in journalism," Evan commented from in front of them.

Moments later, they were at the registration desk. She was already tired, and it wasn't even time for lunch.

After they'd registered, Evan said, "We're just a few rooms apart. I'll pick you up for lunch at twelve-thirty."

She saw that Matt was watching, and she didn't care to create a scene. "Fine. Twelve-thirty."

Upstairs, Paula and Gayle admired their modern and spacious room with its cool garden decor of whites, blues, and greens. In addition to the two queen-sized beds and the usual furniture on the pale green carpeting, there was a raised dining area defined by tall white shutters standing ajar. The nearby windows overlooked the pool, pale beaches, and the shimmering blue sea.

"Why don't you and Evan join us for lunch?" Gayle suggested. "We've seen so little of you."

"I'd love to. I don't know about Evan."

Gayle gave her a sidelong glance. "What's going on between you and Evan? Or is it none of my business?"

"We're only friends," Paula said.

"Maybe you think so," Gayle said, "but you should see the way he gazes at you."

"What do you mean?"

"Josh says Evan looks at you as if you were strawberry ice cream, and Evan were crawling out of the desert."

"Really!" Paula laughed, although on second thought it wasn't so funny. Evan *had* just emerged from a desert of sorts after his divorce.

At twelve-thirty, both Evan and Josh arrived at the door to pick them up.

"Gayle's invited us to have lunch with her and Josh," Paula told Evan. "I hope you don't mind."

Irritation flashed in his eyes for an instant, then he said, "Sure. Why not?"

Josh commented, "Good idea, Gayle."

In the hotel corridor, Paula's heart lurched. In front of them, Matt and Vanessa were walking toward the elevator. Vanessa wore a clinging green strapless dress and her arm was intertwined with his. Could they possibly be sharing a room?

Of course not, Paula reassured herself. Matt and Josh had the room adjacent to Gayle and hers. Vanessa's room was probably just down the hallway since the Santa Rosita group was all on the fourth floor.

"Join us for lunch?" Josh asked them.

Matt turned around, the color in his face deepening as he saw Paula and Evan. "Thanks. We'd like to."

"What's everyone doing today?" Gayle inquired brightly as they stepped into the elevator together.

"We're going shopping," Vanessa replied, still holding Matt's arm. "Aren't we, Matt?" she prompted with an intimate glance.

Gayle remarked, "I'm all for lying out on the beach or around the pool."

"I'm glad to hear it," Josh said as they walked into the hotel's cavernous lobby. "Paula, you're looking terribly tired."

Both Matt and Evan glanced at her.

"And I've been calling *Gayle* a mother hen!" Paula replied.

"I guess that makes me the rooster," Josh said with his lop-sided grin, and they all groaned. He slipped an arm around Gayle, giving her a quick squeeze. "Though I don't mind if she's the hen."

"Never mind that kind of talk!" Gayle laughed with a mischievous look at Josh.

Still chuckling, they arrived at the hotel's colorful Fiesta Restaurant.

As they were seated at a long table, Paula was grateful to see Gayle and Josh take the middle chairs, separating her from Matt and Vanessa.

After studying the menu, Paula said, "You won't believe this, but I'm dying for a hamburger and French fries."

Gayle grinned. "You're not the only one!"

Despite their amusement, the men ordered the same hamburger and French fries plate. Only Vanessa demurred, selecting a chef's salad.

"We can diet when we get home," Gayle said.

Perhaps it's more important for Vanessa to watch her figure since she's older, Paula thought. Vanessa's jet set friends in Cozumel were no doubt fashionably thin. Casting a quick look at Matt, she wondered if he'd go to Cozumel. He seemed unaware of her, admiring the view of the beach and the sea with Vanessa.

152

As they ate their hamburgers and French fries, Paula noticed that Evan was having a third beer. She thought it odd that he and Vanessa never really joined the general conversation. It wasn't as if they were excluded; in fact, Gayle and Josh made special efforts to include them. It seemed more that they wanted to remain on the fringes of the group, that they preferred being outsiders, or didn't understand how to join in.

Still, it was a delightful lunch, Paula thought as they rose to leave.

"Are you sure you don't want to go downtown?" Evan asked her.

"No, thanks. I'm so tired I'd rather just spend a quiet afternoon alone in the sun."

"Fine. If that's what you want, I'll see you for dinner," he said and departed.

For dinner! By the time she collected her wits, it was too late to respond.

Later, as she settled on the white sandy beach, she felt as if someone were watching her. Squinting up into the sun, she saw Evan at the outdoor bar. Hadn't he gone downtown after all? She looked again a few minutes later. He was gone.

Turning with relief toward the turquoise sea, she lay down again and listened to the soft slapping of the waves against the shore. The talcum-soft sand under her orange beach towel was warm, the sound of the sea soothing; she read only a chapter of her paperback novel before drifting off to sleep.

An hour later when a strong breeze came up, she awakened and decided to move to the hotel pool. She found a lounge in the shelter of nearby trees, and there was Evan near the gift shop! Perhaps he hadn't wanted to visit downtown Cancun alone, she thought. Still, he could have joined his co-workers from the computer company. He'd all but abandoned them on the trip lately.

Hours later, after she'd fallen asleep again, Evan tapped her shoulder. "Your back is burning."

She blinked groggily. "I thought you were going downtown."

"Changed my mind," he explained. "We can go tonight before dinner. There are supposed to be some good restaurants and nightclubs. . . ."

How could she possibly refuse him now? It was her own fault for not immediately rejecting his offer of dinner. She could imagine Gayle lecturing her with, "You shouldn't always be so sweet. Sometimes you just have to be firm."

"It's almost five o'clock," Evan said. "Why don't we get ready now?"

She grabbed a deep breath and sat up. How could she still be so tired after resting all afternoon? It wasn't just exhaustion—perhaps it was the humidity as Evan had suggested, but she ached all over too. She'd have to take aspirins in her room.

"Shall we get ready now?" Evan asked again.

"Fine." She suddenly smelled the scent of liquor on his breath.

As Evan helped her out of their taxi in downtown Cancun, Paula was aware of his admiration. Her filmy white dress with its V-neck, long bell sleeves, and full skirt would be flattering to anyone, especially contrasted against a suntan. Evan looked very nice himself in a tan blazer and brown slacks.

He took her arm, and they ambled along the sidewalk, looking at the endless array of shops which offered Yucatec wares—temple rubbings, hand-painted pottery, coral jewelry, tortoiseshell combs, straw hats, and embroidered white clothing—not to mention goods from the rest of Mexico. Men, women, and children vendors bargained with gusto among the tourists.

154

Passing a colorful stall, Paula's eyes were attracted to the coral jewelry.

"Come in, come in, señorita!" the vendor urged.

"Only to look?" she inquired.

"Only to look, señorita," he replied, quickly placing the jewelry at her fingertips. "You like the black from Cozumel or the pink coral?"

"Pink," she answered. She held the earrings to her ears. The price was less than she'd expected. . . .

"We'll take them," Evan said to the vendor, reaching into his jacket pocket for his wallet.

"No—I couldn't possibly let you buy them for me," Paula protested.

Evan was already counting bills out onto the counter. "I *want* to buy them for you." His glance made it clear that he'd feel rejected if she refused him.

The smiling vendor was already accepting the money, and there seemed nothing she could do but to thank Evan and to pay him later.

She slipped on the coral earrings.

"I'll help you with the necklace," Evan said, taking it from the counter and trying to fasten it, his fingers trembling at the nape of her neck. Finally it was fastened, and he stood back to admire her.

She looked at her image in the small mirror on the counter. The coral did look lovely with her blond hair and white dress. "It's beautiful. Thank you, Evan."

His brown eyes were so soft with pleasure that she was glad she'd given in. "You look beautiful," he said proudly. "The most beautiful woman in Cancun."

"It's sweet of you to say so, but I doubt that. I'm not half as beautiful as Vanessa, for example."

"She's not even in your class," he countered. "She looks callous and tough like . . ."

For an instant Paula thought he was going to mention his ex-wife, but he steered her by the elbow instead. "Come on, let's have a drink. We still have an hour until dinner."

Paula shivered, though it had nothing to do with his comment, and the air was still quite warm.

At the restaurant where Evan had made reservations, he checked in with the maître d', who ushered them to the bar. Sitting down, Paula ordered a lemonade. She'd have to take more aspirins for the headache lurking behind her eyes.

Evan ordered a frothy margarita.

When they were served, he offered her a drink from his enormous goblet, its rim edged with salt. "Are you sure you won't try it?"

"No, thanks." She sipped at her lemonade and swallowed the aspirins.

He shrugged and took a long swallow. "Don't you ever drink?"

She shook her head. "I don't care for it." She could have fun without it, she reasoned, although that was the last thing to say now to Evan.

After a few minutes, the maître d' stepped into the bar. "Walker? We have a cancellation if you'd like a table now."

Evan turned to her. "Do you want to eat early?"

"Yes, let's eat now." She wasn't hungry, only so weary that she was anxious to be done with dinner and return to the hotel. What was wrong with her? she fretted, barely able to stand up. She'd never been so tired in her life. She shivered again, attributing it to the air-conditioning.

Inside the restaurant the air was redolent with the scents of broiling meats, but the smells made her nauseous. It seemed forever until their waiter brought the crab hors d'oeuvres, then another eternity until their lobster tail and Mayan steak were presented—the steak in a flaming dish. Food would make her feel better, she told herself. But, delicious as it was, it didn't seem to help. If anything, she felt worse.

By the time dinner was over, she was shivering violently. "Would you mind terribly taking me back to the hotel now, Evan?"

Evan set down his after-dinner liqueur in annoyance. "*Now?*"

"I don't feel well," Paula explained. She touched the back of her hand to her forehead. It was terribly hot.

"But I was hoping to hit some of the nightclubs. There are supposed to be some real live ones. . . ."

"I'm sorry." She couldn't think of anything she'd less like to do. "I don't mind taking a taxi back by myself if you want to stay here."

He glowered at her, then asked for the bill.

Outside the restaurant Evan fumed. "I think I know what your game is. You think that men are free meal tickets—"

"I'm not playing games!" she interrupted. She stepped out to the curb to wave down a taxi. If that's what he thought, she'd much rather go back to the hotel alone. "If you're one of those men who think I owe you something for a dinner, you'll have my money for it—and for the coral jewelry! I'll pay you tomorrow morning when I don't feel like fainting!"

"Listen, Paula . . ."

"I'm sorry I'm being so unpleasant, but I feel very sick!" she explained plaintively, shivering all over.

"Let's just calm down," he suggested, trying to pull her back from the curb.

She twisted away from him, watching for cabs. Two were coming down the street; the first was crowded, but the second cab's overhead light glowed, and she flagged it. "Thanks for a nice dinner, Evan."

He opened the taxi door, helped her in, and climbed in behind her. "Look, I'm sorry if you don't feel well."

She rested her aching head in her hands, too miserable to talk as chills swept through her again and again. He finally seemed to realize that she wasn't acting, but she could scarcely make out his apology. The taxi ride through the dark island with its distant, lighted hotels seemed interminable.

Finally they pulled in at El Pyramide, but she was so weak and feverish that she could scarcely step out of the taxi. Shapes floated, dimmed, then swam into focus.

Evan looked at her in the light of the hotel porte-cochere. "You do look terrible. Here, let me help you."

Leaning on him, she knew that she'd never make it in. They were through the entry doors and in the lobby. Suddenly everything swirled and her body sagged against Evan. She heard him shouting, "Someone, give me a hand!"

When she opened her eyes, everything whirled. Finally she realized she was in bed in her room. Shapes floated before her. After a long while she saw a familiar young man leaning over her and a middle-aged Mexican man wearing a stethoscope around his neck. "I called the hotel doctor," the young man explained.

She attempted to focus on the Mexican's face. A doctor, the other man said.

"Not to worry," the doctor said, his voice seeming to come from a long distance. "I will make you well."

She shivered convulsively. How could her body be so icy cold when her head was burning with fever?

"It's the mosquito bites. Your husband says you have been in Merida."

Her husband? Matt? she wondered. Or was it Tony? But here was . . . ? Evan?

"Do you ache?" the doctor inquired.

"Yes," she managed, her teeth chattering. She had never

ached so in all of her life. It felt as if her bones were bruising her flesh. Things began to come into focus. "I thought it was from climbing the pyramids."

The doctor explained, "It appears that you have denge fever. It is transmitted by the mosquito, like yellow fever and malaria, but not so bad."

"Bad enough!" she muttered through chattering teeth.

"Not to worry," the doctor's voice said, though the words seemed unsynchronized to his lips. "You will feel better after these shots. One is for fever, one antibiotic . . ."

She watched him lift the bedsheet and saw she was wearing only her slip and underwear. Who had undressed her? She ached so hideously that she was only vaguely aware of one shot in her arm, then another.

"It is all over," the doctor stated. "I will leave a prescription for more medicine." He covered her with the sheet again. "You will sleep now," he said in a hypnotic tone. "You will sleep now."

The tenseness drained from her body and, in minutes, she felt warm. The chills were gone. What had he given her to make even her feet and fingers so warm now? She had to strain for his parting words.

"Vaya con Dios."

Surely he didn't mean that she was dying, she thought. *Vaya con Dios* meant "Go with God!"

chapter
9

WHEN PAULA OPENED HER EYES the next morning, she was perplexed by the white, blue, and green room. She lay in a large bed, and across from her in another bed, a red curly-haired head raised up. "Are you feeling better?" Gayle asked.

It took Paula another moment to realize where she was. "Was there a doctor here last night?"

Gayle sat up in her bed. "There certainly was."

"Everything seems so vague, so fragmented."

"I'm not surprised," Gayle replied. "Evan said you collapsed in the lobby and one of the bellboys helped him get you upstairs. They called the hotel doctor. You're apparently a very sick girl."

"I feel weak," she said. She didn't even feel like sitting up. "But I don't ache as badly as last night."

Gayle slipped out of bed and placed her hand on Paula's forehead. "You don't feel quite as feverish now. The doctor's going to stop by again this afternoon. He thinks you have dengue fever from those mosquito bites."

"He's stopping by this afternoon?" That was impossible. "I can't miss the side trip to Tulum," she protested groggily. "I need to take notes. . . ."

"That's the last thing to worry about. Anyhow Matt says you're probably set for the first two articles."

Then Matt knew she was sick too.

"I'm sure that the *Santa Rosita Times* can exist for another twenty or so years without your articles on Cancun and environs," Gayle said with a twinkle in her green eyes.

"I guess it will," Paula admitted with a twinge of amusement. "When am I supposed to start feeling better?"

"Three or four days."

How slowly her mind worked this morning. "What is today?"

"Thursday."

Thursday to Saturday—"That's only *two* days! Saturday we fly home!"

Gayle walked to the window and drew the draperies, letting the morning sunshine flood the room. "You're not to worry about anything. If you're not well enough to fly home, I'll stay with you."

"But you'd lose your tour fare on the plane," Paula objected. "And it would cost you a fortune extra for this room too."

Gayle crossed her arms in a show of firmness. "One of us will be here with you. Matt may stay on to take more pictures, then maybe join Vanessa at Cozumel."

Paula swallowed hard.

"Don't worry." Gayle smiled. "Knowing you, you'll be better in no time. And, if you're not, one of us will stay."

"You can't stay, Gayle."

"You'd do it for me, wouldn't you?"

Paula nodded, her eyes drifting closed. Later, as she wandered in and out of sleep, she wasn't certain whether she'd merely thought or said, "That's what friends are for."

As for friends, she would not count on Matt—or was it Tony? Their images merged in her consciousness, Matt's face sliding over Tony's, then back again until their features were jumbled, confused beyond recognition—Matt suddenly with black hair, Tony with blond. She couldn't depend on either of them, she told herself, but she could depend on Gayle. Yet Gayle didn't have that much money for extra plane fare and the room; she was saving for her wedding.

At noon Paula awakened again. She noticed that Gayle wore a pale green sundress as if ready to go somewhere.

"I'll order consommé for you from room service," Gayle said with a reassuring smile. "You'll be better in no time."

"You've missed your trip to Tulum. I don't want to ruin the rest of the tour for you!"

Gayle shook her red curls and smiled fondly. "You couldn't ruin anything if you tried."

Oh, yes, she could, Paula fretted. She had ruined everything with the men she'd loved, and now she was depriving Gayle and Josh of this trip to Tulum. It was supposed to be a spectacular Mayan ruin, the only one by the sea. "I'll be fine," she insisted. "This isn't fair to Josh." She managed to pull herself into a sitting position. "You and Josh could still go."

Gayle glanced at her watch. "He's checked into renting a car just in case you'd feel better."

"I'm much much better," Paula insisted, mincing the truth. "If you'll just call room service for the consommé—" Inspiration hit. "—and a ham sandwich."

"A ham sandwich!" Gayle repeated. "You *must* be feeling better!"

Paula forced a smile. "You know I never get terribly sick. I probably have a lot more resistance than the doctor thought."

Gayle looked at her doubtfully as she lifted the phone to her ear. After calling room service, she telephoned Josh. "Paula says she feels better. She wants us to go to Tulum." Her voice held a note of dubiousness, but evidently Josh was urging her to go too. When she hung up, she turned again to Paula. "Are you sure you'll be fine?"

163

"Of course!"

"Evan said he'd hang around too," Gayle said. "Well, I'll wait until room service arrives."

It was all Paula could do to maintain her pretense. As for Evan staying around—she saw no reason why he should unless he somehow felt guilty for not bringing her home sooner. What a spectacle she must have made of herself—collapsing in the hotel lobby! Evan had probably been embarrassed.

After room service delivered her lunch, Paula sniffed at the cup of hot beef consommé. It smelled good. She managed to drink it and to nibble away half of the ham sandwich. "I'll save the rest for later," she said, reaching for her paperback novel. "I think I'll read."

"Are you sure?" Gayle asked, looking more and more hopeful.

"Of course! Go and have a good time. You can report it all to me."

Before she left Gayle said, "There are all kinds of juices in our room refrigerator. The doctor says you're to drink lots of liquids. Soft drinks are fine too."

Refrigerator? Paula reflected. Of course, the small hotel refrigerator up in the dining area. She'd seen nuts and other snacks in it too, though it was mostly filled with liquor.

As soon as her roommate departed, Paula sank back down under the covers and fell immediately asleep.

When she awakened again, it was late afternoon. She found Evan standing at her bedside, smiling down at her beside the doctor. How did they get in? Upon reflection, she supposed that the hotel would furnish its doctor with a key. The doctor, whose name she'd already forgotten, asked her questions, and she must have answered because the next time she awakened, he was gone. She had the vague impression that Evan was

164

sitting in the raised dining area by the window, but her eyes fell shut again. In the evening she briefly glimpsed Gayle and Josh—and was that Matt?—in the room.

On Friday morning she insisted that Gayle take the day's trip to Isla Mujeres. "You've already paid for it!" Paula reasoned. She pretended again that she was well before her roommate would go. Once, when awakening, she recalled it was Friday. Tomorrow morning they would be flying home. She had to be well!

When she awakened in the late afternoon, Vanessa stood beside the bed, shaking Paula's shoulder none too gently.

For a moment Paula surmised she was dreaming again. But it was definitely Vanessa and she looked furious.

"I'm not sure whether this is an act you're playing or not," Vanessa began, her voice trembling with fury, "but just because Matt is staying here with you instead of going to Cozumel—"

"Matt's staying on?"

"Spare me your sweet innocence!" Vanessa flared.

"But—"

"Just because he's staying with you, don't suppose it means anything," Vanessa fumed. "After all, I'm the one who taught him everything he knows about women. I know Matt *very well*."

This was another nightmare! Paula decided. But, no, Vanessa's heavy perfume filled the room. Her amber eyes flashed with anger. How could such a beautiful woman possibly be jealous of her?

"As for Matt having the adjoining room and a key . . . ," Vanessa began.

Matt had a key to her room? Did she mean Evan? She had the vague impression that Evan was hovering in the hallway by the door.

"Matt's been in love with me since we were kids," Vanessa continued. "He's taking me to the airport in a few minutes."

Paula blinked in confusion. "Why doesn't he go with you to Cozumel if he's in love with you?"

"Because of you pretending to be sick!" Vanessa exploded, turning on her heel and leaving the room. The door slammed behind her.

The episode became part of a nightmare. Matt and Vanessa were in high school again, walking home holding hands—Matt and Vanessa . . . always Matt and Vanessa.

When she awakened again, it was evening, and there was no one in the room. She had to get up and pack, she thought, dragging herself upright and sitting on the edge of the bed. Finally she stood up. It would be so good to be home in her own bed; she should never have come. Her suitcase lay open on a luggage rack, and she remembered that she had hardly unpacked; there was very little to do but repack her bathing suit and sundress and the white dress she had worn to dinner with Evan. A shower would make her feel better.

In the shower, the spray of hot water stung her body, then she switched on the cold. She must be well for tomorrow; she must go home! When she stepped out into the steamy bathroom, it sounded as if someone opened the door to the room. Slipping into her white terrycloth robe she called out, "Is that you, Gayle?"

No one answered.

She zipped up her robe and opened the bathroom door. No one was in the room. Folding her unpacked clothing, she soon found herself exhausted. She'd lie down for just a moment.

When she opened her eyes again, Evan was sitting across the room in the dining area by the window, a paperback novel in hand. Apparently aware of her awakening, he set the book on the table near the empty liquor bottles. He was now drinking what appeared to be red wine.

"How did you get in here?" she asked sleepily, pulling up the covers to her neck as she sat up. Perhaps it was thoughtful of him to sit with her, but it made her feel uneasy.

Instead of answering he replied, "You must be feeling better. You showered."

How did he know? Unless—unless he'd come in while she was in the shower, when she thought she'd heard the door. It crossed her mind that he must have a key. Could it be from the night when she had fainted in the lobby? The doctor had thought Evan was her husband; perhaps a desk clerk had assumed so too. Or perhaps he'd automatically handed out a key during the excitement and had forgotten about it.

Evan leaned back in his chair, observing her closely. "I think that you feel a lot better than you let on."

"Why on earth would you say that?" she inquired, thinking she heard a door close in Matt's room. If only Matt would come to check on her!

Evan raised his eyebrows. "Isn't—isn't it true?"

"It's most certainly not true that I'm pretending! Why should I?"

He drained his wineglass before answering. "Maybe because you want Matt to stay alone with you here."

"What a thing to say!" Had Evan been drinking even before he arrived in her room? If so, he'd had quite a lot. "Do you think it's fun for me to miss all of the trips—not to mention my note-taking?"

He stared at her. "Don't think you fool me! You've always been in love with that stupid Matt Montgomery! Everyone in Santa Rosita knows it except him!"

She closed her eyes in resignation. Had she been that obvious? She managed, "I appreciate your concern, Evan, but if you'd leave now . . ."

167

"I'm not leaving," he contended, sitting back comfortably. He filled his wine glass again, rambling on about how he'd given up his afternoon to keep an eye on her.

How slurred his words were becoming! Of course, he was drunk—he'd said his ex-wife had a drinking problem. Why hadn't she guessed that he did too?

Paula spoke as evenly as possible. "This *is* my room, Evan. I didn't invite you in, and I didn't want you to sit here all afternoon. If you don't mind, I'd like some privacy now. I'd like you to leave."

"To leave!" he flared. "After all of my trouble . . ."

The thing to do was to firmly usher him out, she told herself. Aware that she still wore her white terrycloth robe, she stood up weakly. "Evan, if you don't leave, I'll call the desk clerk." The growing anger on Evan's face stopped her.

She hardly knew what to do as he came to his feet. He was turning redder and redder. "Evan—?"

"Tease!" he shouted.

Paula reached for the telephone on the nightstand as he stepped down from the dining area. As she pressed the button for the hotel operator, Evan strode across the room.

"Operator . . . ," a voice responded.

Fury boiled in Evan's bloodshot eyes. There was no time to explain anything to the operator, to anyone. As Evan vaulted across Gayle's bed toward her Paula shouted, "Matt Montgomery's room!" Dropping the phone, she ran between the beds to escape out the door but Evan grabbed her shoulder, twisting her to him.

"Leave me alone!" she cried out. "You're hurting me!"

His eyes glittered vengefully before he crushed her against his chest. "I'm not leaving you alone anymore! I'm tired—tired of being a gentleman! What you need is someone—someone who knows how to love a woman—"

168

Struggling, she cried out, "Matt!"

Evan slapped her face hard.

"Matt!" she screamed again hopelessly, remembering he'd taken Vanessa to the airport. She grappled with Evan, but he was amazingly strong. "Matt! Help me!"

The adjoining door burst open, and Matt rushed in, towering over them as he tore Evan away. "Get out of here!" he shouted, grabbing the shorter man with such fury that Evan's brown eyes bulged.

Evan broke away and aimed a punch at Matt's chin, but missed, and Matt twisted Evan's arms behind him. "Don't you ever go near Paula again!" He was furious.

Paula thought this must be another of her dreams! Now Matt was wrestling Evan out of the room. It occurred to her—"Evan has my room key!"

When Matt returned, he shut the door behind him, locking it and breathing hard. Darting a glance at her, he placed Evan's key on the dresser. "He doesn't have it anymore." As he turned to her, his face was full of concern. "Are you all right now?"

She realized that she was trembling with shock. "If you hadn't been there! If you hadn't come!" Maybe Matt thought it was all her fault. "Truly, I didn't encourage him!"

Quite suddenly she was sobbing, and Matt caught her in a protective embrace. "It's all right, Paula. It's all right," he repeated over and over. After a while, he patted her back as if she were a little girl.

It reminded her of when she was a child and had skinned her knee while he babysat her. Nothing had changed!

"He won't bother you anymore. They'll all be leaving tomorrow," Matt assured her.

"I thought you'd taken Vanessa to the airport . . . that you weren't back," Paula sobbed.

"She took a taxi," he said, stroking her hair softly. "It's all right now."

Slowly she felt her body relaxing. Finally she caught her breath and sat on the edge of the bed, certain she hadn't cried as much as this last week in all of her life. How could everything have gone so wrong?

Matt felt her forehead. "Has the doctor been here today?"

She shook her head.

"I think I'd better call him. You get into bed."

"He thought that Evan was my—my husband," Paula remembered as she slipped into her bed.

"That's one mistake he won't make again!" Matt said with vehemence. After a moment he added, "Try to sleep. I'll leave the door between our rooms open. Gayle got me a key for when they're all gone. I hope you don't mind."

"I trust you," she said quite simply.

He gave her a slow grin. "Thanks. I suppose that's a compliment."

"It is," she acknowledged, though she didn't trust him in all respects. She was certain he wouldn't abuse her physically, but she didn't trust him with her heart anymore.

When the doctor arrived, Matt answered the door and spoke to him in the hallway for a few moments.

"Here's the doctor," he said, then retreated to his own room.

The doctor appeared a bit perplexed, but after examining her said, "One more shot. It will make you very sleepy. You must rest and not overexert yourself."

She nodded. Why bother explaining that she'd overexerted herself to fight off Evan? It was all too complicated. She was nearly asleep when the doctor departed. The last thing she saw was Matt's concerned face.

"Should I leave the adjoining door open until Gayle comes back?" he asked.

Paula nodded groggily.

Dozing off, she dreamed of the time she had brought him the roses. How handsome he was with his sun-streaked blond hair. He was gazing at the roses in astonishment. "Hasn't anyone ever given you flowers?" she asked as if it were an everyday event for her to bring roses to a man. She smiled up at him and, for a wondrous moment, they were encircled by the fragrance of the roses and the warmth of the sunshine shimmering through the trees.

"Not anyone so beautiful," he had said.

chapter
10

GAYLE STRUGGLED TO SHUT her suitcase on the pale green carpeting. "Just consider your staying on as an added vacation," she suggested to Paula. "It'll only be four or five days."

"A blessing in disguise?" Paula asked ruefully as she sat on the edge of her bed in her blue nightie and peignoir.

She wished that she were more like Gayle, accepting the aggravations of life more gracefully. As for additional vacation, the extra cost of the hotel and airfare would finish her savings entirely. Moreover, there was nothing holidaylike about staying behind with Matt. Last night after so furiously evicting Evan, Matt had conducted himself as if she were still the little girl next door. He'd soothed and consoled her, but evidently there'd been no romance for him in embracing her now.

So far, nothing about denge fever vaguely resembled a blessing. This morning she had managed to brush her teeth and shower, but still didn't have the energy to get dressed. The only good thing that came to mind was that Evan was leaving this morning with the rest of the Santa Rosita group.

She watched Gayle wrestling with her suitcase and finally had to smile. Between Gayle's clothing and her purchases, there seemed little hope of holding the suitcase shut. "I'll sit on it for you," Paula offered. "It's not the first time."

"Super!" Gayle gave the contents a final shove away from the edges. "Ready?"

The moment the lid was down, Paula sat on it.

"Voilà!" Gayle exclaimed, snapping shut the locks.

Josh knocked at their adjoining door. "Are you two decent?" he asked.

"Maybe not decent, but dressed," Gayle laughed, inserting the key into the suitcase locks. "You can come in."

"So that's how you get it shut," Josh chuckled as he walked in. He dropped a kiss on Gayle's forehead. "I'll put the suitcase out in the hallway for you. Are you set to go down to breakfast?"

"Could I meet you down in the coffee shop in a few minutes?" Gayle suggested. "I'm not quite ready."

"Sure," Josh answered good-naturedly, and Paula wished again that she had such a comfortable relationship with a man who loved her.

As Josh carried out the suitcase, he called back to Paula, "If I don't see you until we're back in Santa Rosita, take care of yourself. We'll be at the airport to pick you up."

"Thanks so much, Josh," Paula responded gratefully.

"Our pleasure," he replied.

When he was gone Paula turned to Gayle. "Do you have any idea of how lucky you are to have someone like Josh?"

Gayle shook her auburn curls as she packed her carry-on case and a white plastic bagful of purchases. "Luck has nothing to do with it. Josh is an out-and-out blessing from the Lord."

"You believe that, don't you?" Paula inquired.

"I sure do. I prayed for someone like Josh, and not two days later, there he was at a church dinner with his parents.

He thought he was there to hear the speaker, but the Lord wanted us to meet. Josh thinks so too in retrospect."

Paula sank dejectedly on her bed. "I prayed too, Gayle," she began. "I prayed in a little church in Piste, and here's what's happened: first, I got denge fever, and then Evan attacked me!" She didn't even want to mention the worst—that Vanessa had taken over Matt.

Gayle paused in her packing. "Surely you don't think that God made you sick or caused Evan to attack you?"

"I don't know. . . ."

"Honey, the reason you have trouble understanding is that you've never committed yourself unreservedly to Jesus. And I do mean *unreservedly*. Sure, you used to go to church, but you just tiptoed around the edges of faith. It's not enough to believe now and then, or just when you're in trouble. . . ."

"And have you committed yourself so unreservedly?" Paula returned with annoyance.

Gayle nodded solemnly. "Yes. When my father died and I didn't care about even living anymore . . . when it didn't seem possible for us to go on without him, I finally gave my entire life over to Jesus—and I've never regretted it."

"I'm sorry . . . I didn't realize . . . ," Paula began, remembering so many years ago when Gayle's father had died of a sudden heart attack. He had been the light of her life, beloved by the whole community. "I suppose I'd have been furious with God."

"Oh, I was at first! I was especially mad because Dad had been such a great believer. I kept saying, 'It's not fair, God! It's not fair!'"

"Well, it wasn't fair, Gayle!"

"No one has ever promised us that life would be fair . . . or what we might think is fair. But what I eventually discovered through all of it was that God gives us the strength to handle anything that can happen to us. I lean very heavily on Philippians 4:13 . . . *I can do all things through Christ, who strengtheneth me.*"

"I see," Paula said, although she was not certain that she did. Strange that they'd known each other so well for all of these years, and she'd never understood how her best friend had arrived at her faith.

Gayle glanced at her watch. "I'd better run. But I do want to assure you that God did not send a mosquito after you! And he didn't send Evan after you either!" She gave Paula a big hug. "God is all good . . . he's love . . . he loves you even more than I do!"

Before Paula could answer, her roommate rushed for the door. "See you at the airport!"

"Tell everyone good-bye from me!" Paula called after her.

Climbing back into bed, she felt slightly miffed about their religious discussion, but then she *had* been curious.

At noon there was a knock on the connecting door. "It's Matt," he said. "May I come in?"

Paula tugged up the covers. "Come in." Fortunately, the maid had already changed Gayle's bed and cleaned the room.

He looked a trifle embarrassed. "If I'd knocked on the front door you'd have had to get up."

"It's all right," she assured him. "I feel very bad about your staying here with me though."

"Nonsense," he protested with a bright smile. "I wanted to get more pictures of Cancun anyhow. The tour went far too rapidly to really get enough good shots."

Paula returned his smile. "Then I don't have to feel guilty?"

"You don't have to feel guilty." He glanced around the room, then apparently decided it was suitable to sit on the edge of Gayle's bed. "I'm a little uneasy about leaving you alone after last night. I thought you might be nervous. . . ."

"Nervous?" Could that be why he'd treated her so carefully last night, why her being in his arms had been no more than a protective embrace? An appalling idea flashed to mind. "Didn't Evan leave with the others?"

"He's gone," Matt assured her. "I went downstairs to see everyone off this morning."

She felt relieved, then a twinge of gratefulness that the trip wasn't over for her too. Maybe . . . No, she didn't want to even hope. . . . "I don't want you sitting around in your room. . . ."

"You need peace of mind, a feeling of security while you rest," he responded.

"It's thoughtful of you, Matt, and I'm thankful you're staying on, but I don't want you to sit around nearby all day because of me."

"Oh, I've been busy," he insisted. "I jogged along the beach this morning before everyone left and took some wonderful pictures of daybreak. Besides the dawn shots over the Caribbean, I got some of colorful little tropical birds along the beaches."

"Sounds lovely," she replied, aware that he was trying to sidetrack her objection. "But the fact remains that since everyone left, you've been sitting in your room—babysitting me again! I don't have a fever this morning, and I'll probably sleep this afternoon. If you sit around anymore, I *will* feel guilty."

He laughed. "I've never been known for being too idle. I've been researching the area to see where I might want to take pictures." He glanced toward her stack of folders and brochures on the dresser. "Do you suppose I might borrow some of your material?"

"Certainly. But you're not allowed to feel responsible for me now. No one's going to break in, and according to the doctor, I'm not apt to die of this."

"I know," he admitted, "but I feel like we're—we're old friends."

"Thanks." She remembered their passionate kisses. Those moments she'd considered rapture he'd apparently considered being old friends!

"Why don't I call room service to bring up some lunch for us?" he suggested.

"I absolutely refuse to allow you to have lunch here."

He finally gave in, but was adamant about dinner. "We'll have the best dinner in the house sent up," he promised. "Sleep and get well!"

"I will," Paula replied, and moments after he'd left the room, she slept.

At four-thirty she awakened, feeling strong enough to wash her hair and to change into her new hand-embroidered cotton caftan. Later, when she examined herself in the mirror, her blond hair gleamed, and her eyes were bright with excitement instead of fever.

At six o'clock Matt knocked at their adjoining door.

"Come in!" she called from the dining area where she was reading. It seemed the only decorous place in the room to meet him.

"You're up!" he remarked. "And looking so much better."

For an instant she remembered that morning in the Merida hotel room when he'd come into her room behind the bellboy. What was it Matt had told her? Something about never letting a man into her room again, and then *he'd* swept her into his arms. The memory made her blush.

"You're not feverish again?" he inquired.

She placed a hand on her forehead. It was warm, normal. "I'm fine," she answered. Only foolish to dwell on memories. He was probably anxious to join Vanessa!

"When are you leaving for Cozumel?" she asked.

"I don't know. It depends."

Depends on what? she wondered.

Matt telephoned in their dinner order from the room service menu: cream of asparagus soup, salads, Mayan steaks, and flan. Ordering steaks reminded Paula of the dinner she'd eaten in downtown Cancun with Evan—the steaks arriving in ceremonial flames at their elegant table and the evening ending in ashes with her collapse in the lobby.

After a time, the room service waiter arrived without ceremony or flames; he lighted the dining area's chandelier with a flip of the electric switch, set the table with white linen tablecloth and napkins, served their dinner, and discreetly disappeared.

Evening was falling as Matt seated her. He sat down across the table, and she turned nervously to the cream of asparagus soup.

"It's full of fresh asparagus, the way I make it," Matt commented.

"You make asparagus soup?" Paula returned in amazement. "I thought you weren't domestic."

"Now where did you get that idea?" he asked.

"At Gayle's house, the night she and Josh prepared dinner."

Matt chuckled at the memory. "Josh and I just like to give each other a bad time. I'm a fairly decent cook."

"I can't believe it!"

He seemed taken aback at her astonishment. "It's not nearly as wonderful as advertised to eat in restaurants all of the time. I've been living alone for nearly eight years now, since I moved into my first apartment."

Living alone? She'd supposed that he hadn't lived alone at all.

"You didn't think that I'd eaten in restaurants all eight years?" he asked.

"I guess I'd never thought about it quite like that."

She did know that Tony would never stoop to cooking. Although he'd never admitted it, he'd clearly considered cooking to be "women's work." As for cleaning up, he'd made a big show of how liberated he was by carrying his dishes to the kitchen sink, then quickly exiting.

"Have you ever eaten in a restaurant alone?" Matt asked.

"No . . . not in an elegant restaurant."

He sighed. "The sympathetic stares are enough to lay you low."

"I suppose they would." She'd assumed that he lived a glamorous life in a whirl of nightclubs and restaurants. Hadn't his own mother called him a playboy?

"It's honey celery seed," Matt said.

"Honey celery seed?" she inquired, then realized he was talking about the salad dressing. She tasted the slightly sweet dressing, dubbed a house specialty by the hotel menu. "You do know," she responded, trying to pretend that they weren't in her bedroom. The setting made her nervous.

Finally she said into the awkward silence, "I'm having such a difficult time believing that you actually cook, though I suppose you learned to make hot dogs and hamburgers in your scouting days."

His blue eyes held hers with a heart-stopping intensity. "I'm not a scout anymore, Paula."

She was so disconcerted by his gaze that she only said, "I know." His kisses made that quite clear. From the warmth in his eyes it occurred to her that he might be remembering too.

She decided to shift their conversation to safer ground. "Wouldn't our parents enjoy being here?"

He shook his head. "Mine don't especially like to travel. Dad was in Europe during World War II, and he vowed that if he came home alive he'd never leave California again. I don't think he has. Yet, as you know, they've probably explored every beach, lake, and mountain in the state."

"Strange. And our generation is so wild to see the world." She wondered if Matt's father had made a vow to God about coming home alive. The Montgomerys had long attended the same neighborhood church that her own parents had recently joined. As for traveling, her mother and father enjoyed it occasionally, but it wasn't the most important interest in their lives.

"You don't much like men, do you?" Matt suddenly asked.

"Why I— Of course I do!" What made him ask that? Did it have to do with Evan last night, or did he know about Tony? Still, she liked men very well, she reassured herself before an inner voice asked, *"But do you trust them?"*

"Josh said that you walked out of a difficult situation when you left Phoenix."

"Yes," she replied hesitantly. "Yes, I did."

"It seems that we all do at one time or another," he said rather stiffly.

"I suppose so," she agreed, looking at her plate. No doubt he referred to Vanessa walking out on him years ago as well.

Paula cut into her tender steak with its mushrooms, peppers, and onions, and put a forkful in her mouth. Barely aware of its delectable flavor, she stared blindly at the rice, black beans, and cheese-topped baked tomato on the plate. At last she spoke again to fill the silence. "Now don't tell me you make Mayan steak."

He chuckled. "Not yet."

The conversation became more comfortable as they turned to their childhood memories of Santa Rosita. After a while Paula found herself saying, "I remember when Gayle and I ran after you on your bicycle when you delivered the *Santa Rosita Times*. You must have detested us."

"Not so much," he replied. "I wasn't smart enough to know a good thing when I saw it."

She laughed. "You were smart enough to avoid us as much as possible!"

Tasting her flan, a delicious custardy dessert with brown sugar, she looked out the window at the lighted swimming pool and the hotel grounds; beyond, the sandy beaches and the blue sea were almost lost in the night. Above her, the chandelier turned the dining area into an island of light—and her bedroom to their side, like the sea, nearly disappeared in the semidarkness. Nearly, but not quite. She sat back after she'd finished her flan, unsure of what to do.

Matt rose from the table, smiling at her. "I'd better let you get your rest. You still look pale under that tan."

She stood up. "Maybe I'll read for a while. Gayle bought me a new paperback. . . ."

Matt started for the connecting door to his room, and she trailed after him uneasily. "Shall I leave the door unlocked in case you feel bad in the night?" he offered.

"Oh, no!" she replied far too quickly. "I'll be just fine." She suspected that he was hiding a smile. "Thank you for a lovely dinner, Matt."

"My pleasure. Maybe tomorrow you can lie out by the pool. And, just in case you make a miraculous recovery, I've made reservations for us at The Yucatecan, the best restaurant in the hotel."

"But—"

"But nothing," he protested. "You'll only be allowed to go if you're feeling much better. It's supposed to be an incentive."

"Thanks, Matt," she replied.

"Good night, Paula." His blue eyes moved quickly away from hers.

"Good night." She watched the door close behind him and was glad to hear him turn the key in the lock. He could just as easily unlock it, but she knew that he wouldn't unless she called him.

The next day Matt refused to leave her. As they found chaise lounges out by the hotel pool he said, "I'm feeling too lazy today. Besides you'll be up and around by tomorrow. The doctor said three or four more days. Just look at how much you've improved already."

"I do feel better," she admitted, taking off her white terrycloth beach cover-up.

She lay down on the chaise in her one-piece blue bathing suit, aware that Matt was admiring her trim figure. It occurred to her that the last time he'd seen her in a bathing suit was two weeks ago at the neighborhood pool. How long ago that seemed now.

He settled on the adjacent lounge. "If you're feeling well enough tomorrow, I thought we might go to Tulum. I can rent a car, and it's an easy drive. There's a national park nearby too that we're not supposed to miss. Xel-ha."

She slathered herself with suntan lotion, wondering if he wasn't more anxious to join Vanessa in Cozumel. "But it's not fair to you to have to stay just because I'm ill."

"If you syndicate the first two travel articles, the one on Cancun and the surrounding area will be in demand. It's a natural follow-up."

"I suppose so, though I'll never get rich on that!"

"I wouldn't mind the travel credits for my pictures if you get the article syndicated all over the country," he remarked. "It would make my travel books more attractive to prospective publishers if I had a number of newspaper credits."

He seemed serious about it, and she did want to go.

The mid-morning sunshine beamed all around them and soft music swirled across the pool from the thatch-roofed refreshment bar. A sense of well-being swept through her, and she turned to him with a hopeless smile. "You're very convincing."

"I'd hoped so," he said. "You'll go?"

She wished that he hadn't donned his dark glasses so that she might see the look in those blue eyes. Yet she rather enjoyed the sense of mystery the sunglasses imparted. "I'll go," she replied.

At one o'clock, they ambled to the outdoor dining room overlooking the turquoise sea. Sitting at a narrow table, she felt the balmy air soothe away her sense of caution. She felt more and more drawn to him as they sat eating chef's salads and listening to the sound of the waves curling to the white sandy beach.

"Time for your nap," he said after lunch. "I'll go upstairs with you. I have to make a call."

She thought nothing of it.

On the crowded hotel elevator, someone jostled her against Matt, and she felt an electrifying attraction to him. Looking up, she realized he was aware of the magnetism between them too. If only Vanessa hadn't walked back into his life!

They were strangely silent walking to her room. At her door Matt turned to her uneasily. "Try to rest. I'll pick you up at six for dinner."

"Fine—"

"Paula . . . ?" His low voice was husky with emotion.

Down the corridor, a door closed and an elderly couple started toward them.

"Yes?"

"Nothing," he replied. "Only wear a pretty dress."

She was fairly certain that he'd had *something* in mind

before the couple appeared on the scene. She unlocked her door and darted a shy smile at him. "I will."

Minutes before six o'clock, Paula waited in her room. She'd slept for two hours and was rested, but now she brimmed with anticipation. She examined herself in the full-length mirror. Her deep blue dress with its diaphanous pleated bell sleeves and overskirt was the prettiest she'd ever owned; its V-neck was demure yet enchanting. It looked like a dress for dancing on a moonlit terrace. In the mirror, her face glowed; her eyes were clear again, bluer than ever.

At six, Matt knocked at the corridor door. When she opened it, his eyes widened with appreciation. "You're certainly wearing something pretty," he observed.

"Thank you," she laughed. "I tried."

She was pleased that she'd never worn the dress with Tony. He liked her to wear black dresses, to look sophisticated, not like an innocent, as he called it.

In the Yucatecan, romantic music wafted across the candlelit room. Paula and Matt sat in a plush green leather corner booth while their waiter prepared a Caesar salad before them as if officiating at a sacred rite; he later flamed the huge prawns for their entrée with matching solemnity. Paula restrained a smile.

"The rituals amuse you, don't they?" Matt asked.

Paula's honesty asserted itself. "It's interesting to watch, but they seem to take it so seriously. Sometimes I'm tempted to giggle. Is it really that important to them?"

Matt chuckled. "My sentiments precisely. I suppose most of us are rather amusing when we're too fervent about our work."

"Tell me about your work," she suggested. "About how you happened to start the company."

185

"You really want to know?" he asked.

"I really do!"

Slowly his story unfolded. Just graduated from Stanford, he'd begun with nothing more than his education and determination when he'd started the electronics company. It had taken off like a rocket, despite his peers' doubts. Finally, it had grown so rapidly that it consumed his life. "Yet it didn't bring me happiness," he explained. "I decided there must be something better to living than just working and spending money."

"Oh?" Everyone had always raved about his fantastic success. She'd never suspected that he'd been unhappy.

After a while she found herself telling him about her public relations job in Phoenix, skirting the issue of Tony and explaining her actual work.

"You didn't like it, did you?" Matt guessed.

"No, not really. It was too much gilding of the lily for me, and too many of the so-called lilies—the clients—were out-and-out thorns. There's really nothing that I enjoy as much as writing about people and places, but with honesty."

"Then you should," Matt said. "You should use your gift the way it was intended."

Her gift? She'd never considered her writing ability as a gift. As for how it was intended—she hadn't really thought about that either. She'd have to give the idea some thought.

After dinner they strolled around the hotel, looking in on the shops, then sitting in the darkness by the pool. Stars sparkled in the moonlit sky, and a soft breeze whispered through the palm trees. As they chatted about the scenery, the passers-by, and the day ahead, strange undercurrents flowed between their words and silences.

"Paula . . . ?" Matt began. Moonlight shimmered across his golden hair as he bent toward her, taking her hand in his.

186

"Yes, Matt?" she asked.

It was a long time until he spoke, and by then his tone of voice had become casually distant. "We'd better get you in so you're well tomorrow to go to Tulum."

Regret swept through her. Surely he'd begun with something very different in mind, she thought as he tugged her lightly to her feet.

At her door he asked, "Shall we leave early for Tulum? Nine? Ten?"

"Nine is fine," she answered, then laughed at her inadvertent rhyming. Eight would be better. Even seven. Or six! She couldn't seem to get enough of being with him. But what was new about that?

Pleasant morning drive in Matt's air-conditioned rental car, Paula jotted in her notebook, not mentioning the excitement throbbing through her. *The white limestone road cuts through low green jungle like a ribbon leading to adventure. Occasional windmills protrude over the tropical vegetation, usually near Mayan settlements.*

As they stopped to look at a chicle tree from the car window, she read from her guidebook, "People came in search of chicle trees for making chewing gum and found the Mayan ruins here instead."

Matt chuckled. "Just like life. Looking for one thing and finding another."

Like her own embarking on this trip to forget Tony and discovering that she still loved Matt, she brooded. Her heart felt a twinge of anguish as she remembered she'd be flying home, and Matt would be flying to Vanessa in Cozumel.

The parking lot at Tulum was jammed with tour buses. Tourists moved slowly among the native shops, many sipping soft drinks from cans and some using straws to drink milk from coconuts.

187

As they strolled to the fieldstone gate leading to the ruins of the ancient walled city, the air was oppressive. "Are you going to be all right?" Matt asked.

"I think so." She already felt limp.

"We'll take our time. You can sit down if you like."

"I'll be fine," she insisted, but Matt looked at her dubiously before he went to buy tickets.

Minutes later, they were inside the gate, and Paula caught her breath at the sight. The Mayan ruins rising from the land were extensive and very different from any others they had seen—lower structures, no pyramids. She and Matt made their way to the main buildings, surrounded by groups of tourists and guides speaking English, Spanish, French, and German. Paula caught bits of the talks. "Post-classic Maya. Temples and palaces were low—a time of the Mayan decline."

Here and there were remnants of primitive paintings on the ruins in black, red, blue, and green. "No carvings in Tulum," another guide explained.

"How this must have impressed the Spaniards," Paula said, glancing at the remnants of its castle, watchtower, and temple.

When she and Matt had finally wandered through the ruins to the sea cliff, the view over the tropical growth and out to the turquoise sea was magnificent. Matt climbed up and down the ancient stairways and cliffs to take pictures, and Paula sat down on the sand with her notebook. Her mind seemed to capture the vision that had come to the Spaniards who had first seen Tulum.

She began to write: *Here at the Mayan's "city of dawn," traders once glided by in huge canoes laden with jade, honey, wax, salt, and feathers. The first Mayan city sighted by the Spaniards, Tulum must have impressed them with its castle, watchtower and Temple of Frescoes. They described it as being as large as Seville.*

She wrote on, caught up in the wonder and beauty of the place, delighted that her research had merged with what she saw now. She was blissfully unaware of the passing tourists or the bright sunshine and humidity.

After a long time, she realized that she had written the entire section on Tulum for her article; it had nearly written itself. When she looked up, Matt was sitting on the sand beside her.

"You look as pleased as I feel about the pictures," he commented.

"Wonderful!" She allowed him to help her up.

At the shops on the edge of the parking lot, they stopped for iced colas. "If you have enough energy, we can stop at Xel-ha for lunch," Matt suggested. "It's on the way."

"I'm fine. I wouldn't miss it," Paula insisted, though she felt wobbly. She didn't want to ruin his day. And now that her Cancun area article was actually underway, she had to see that famous national park and natural aquarium.

When they arrived at Xel-ha, a breeze blew through the trees. It rippled the brilliantly hued water and caressed the white sandy beaches above rocky shores. "It's magnificent!" she exclaimed, taking notes. "I didn't expect this!"

Matt took pictures at every turn.

In a huge open thatch-roofed restaurant, they lunched on buttery lobster, black beans, and hot corn tortillas. "Another feast," she pronounced. "I'll get fat."

"I doubt that," Matt said, taking another appreciative look at her. She'd worn a white sundress over her bathing suit, and the way he gazed at her made her feel beautiful.

A cruise ship had anchored in the distant bay and tendered passengers across to the white beaches, where they sat under trees eating their box lunches. Snorkelers explored the turquoise water off the rocky shore.

"Let's rent a boat," Matt suggested and she agreed. It would be a rest.

They wandered to the small pier to make arrangements. After a while, an oarsman rowed toward them and helped them aboard, then the three of them glided across the shimmering lagoon. The surrounding low jungle was just across the water, and above, the sky was azure with puffy white clouds. In the shallower water, the surface was so clear and mirror-smooth that it served as a window to view the brilliant tropical fish.

"Far too lovely for note-taking," Paula said, glancing at Matt. It seemed that they were in paradise.

Later they lay on the white sandy beach in their bathing suits, and despite the beauty of the scene, Paula's eyes drifted shut. She slept deeply for a long time, then the dream came to her. She and Matt were on a small boat, gliding across the lagoon; his blue eyes brimmed so with love that words were unnecessary. In the midst of their happiness Vanessa appeared behind him, her lovely hand gripping his shoulder, twisting him away to her.

"Matt's always loved me!" Vanessa said angrily. "He always has, and he always will!"

"No!" Paula cried. "No!"

When she opened her eyes, Matt was gently shaking her shoulder. "You're dreaming, Paula," he said. "What on earth was that about?"

Blinking, she found only Matt. She sat up and groggily brushed the sand from her arms. "I was dreaming—" She stopped abruptly.

"About what?"

"Nothing much. Thanks for waking me up."

As she looked out again at the beauty of Xel-ha, the dream finally receded.

"It's nearly four o'clock," Matt told her at length. "I'd better get you back to the hotel if we're to go to Isla Mujeres tomorrow."

"I'd hate to miss it. If only life could continue like this. . . ." *Forever,* she'd nearly said.

When they returned to the hotel, she was still brushing the remnants of sand from her arms while they stepped into the elevator. "It was such a wonderful day," she remarked to Matt as the elevator started up.

His eyes gleamed with warmth. "It was for me too."

Moments later, as the elevator door opened on their floor, Paula couldn't believe her eyes.

Vanessa Starke Packard!

The dark-haired beauty stood poised to enter the elevator, but stepped back when she saw them. "There you are!" she exclaimed at Matt. "After your phone call yesterday, I decided that things were rather dull in Cozumel."

Paula's heart sank. Matt had phoned her?

Vanessa's amber eyes darted curiously toward Paula, then back to him, and Paula understood precisely why Vanessa had returned. She was not taking any chances on losing him!

chapter
11

AT EIGHT-THIRTY THE NEXT MORNING, Paula waited in the shade of a thatch-roofed bus stop with Matt, Vanessa, and three couples from their hotel. A warm breeze rustled the palm fronds overhead, and small yellow birds twittered from the nearby hibiscus. Just beyond Paseo Kukulkan, the nearly trafficless main highway, the Caribbean Sea shimmered bright turquoise and blue. Paula felt almost well again, and the glorious sun-drenched day seemed so full of promise for their boat trip to Isla Mujeres . . . and so full of decision.

She glanced at Vanessa in her scanty white shorts and strapless top. She was gorgeous with her dark hair, amber eyes, and voluptuous figure, like an exotic tropical bird. By comparison, Paula thought she must look like an ingénue in her sedate blue sundress. If only Vanessa hadn't shown up!

"Here it comes!" Matt exclaimed. He hurried out to the highway to flag the bus. He'd seemed in a holiday mood since breakfast, as if it weren't unusual for him to escort two women around. Last night he'd seemed a trifle uneasy squiring them to a restaurant, though he'd tried to create a pleasant atmosphere. After dinner, the three of them had strolled through the gift shops and out around the pool. Matt had been the one to suggest turning in early. At least, Paula had hoped that Matt and Vanessa had turned in early—and separately.

As the bus slowed for them, Vanessa laughed. "How terribly chic to ride the local bus when you have a rental car at the hotel!"

Matt shrugged. "When you collaborate on travel articles, you have to try out the transportation that other tourists might use."

"To be perfectly honest," Vanessa replied, "I'd feel better if we'd chartered our own boat. You never know quite what to expect on excursion boats or local buses."

Paula found herself objecting. "But if you didn't take local buses and excursions, you'd never meet the natives, nor have any real adventures."

Vanessa shot her a contemptuous look, as if to say, "What could one expect from anyone so untraveled?"

Matt seemed unaware of their interchange.

First to board the bus, Vanessa saved a seat beside her. "Over here," she called out to Matt.

"Thanks, but this is better," he answered, sitting behind the bus driver in the aisle-facing seat. "I'm supposed to tell him where we get off to catch the boat."

A quick smile masked Vanessa's anger. "In *your* Spanish?"

"I'll manage," Matt answered with a grin. "Come sit here with us."

"No, thanks," Vanessa replied petulantly.

Settling down next to him, Paula said nothing, noticing that Vanessa's smile faded as Matt talked to the bus driver.

As Matt sat back he remarked in a quiet tone, "This beats driving. Besides, I turned in the car."

"Oh?" Paula replied, surprised that he'd confided in her. Why hadn't he told Vanessa? Would she expect a car at her beck and call?

Paula extracted her notebook from her shoulder bag. As she began to take notes about the changing scenery, Matt read over her shoulder. She said, "I hope you can read my scribbling better than I can!"

"For a bus writer, you scribble very neatly," he responded, his breath warm in her hair.

Remembering their kisses, she glanced up into his eyes. They met hers, glowing with warmth. Her heart raced, and after a fast smile, she quickly turned to her notebook. If only she weren't so frightened of being hurt again now!

After a while she glanced up at Vanessa, who smiled coolly, as if she wasn't in the least concerned about what was taking place between them. Her air of self-confidence was more than disconcerting. How could the woman be so self-assured unless she knew something Paula didn't know?

A grayness of suspicion descended upon her like a cloud, and negative thoughts pierced her consciousness: Maybe Matt was trying to make Vanessa jealous—Tony had used her in that precise way to make his wife jealous. Maybe it was a common male game—something men did to feed their egos.

No! She thrust the thoughts away. There was nothing to be gained from pessimism, especially since she'd promised herself to be open to whatever might happen today.

Last night in her room after dinner, she'd decided it was too late to unravel her tangled trail of mistakes with Matt. If he preferred Vanessa by the end of the day, she'd fly home alone tomorrow morning. She'd called the airport last night, and there'd be no difficulty in obtaining a seat on the morning plane. Still, she would wait; she would give the future she'd dreamed of with him this one last day.

She was jerked back to the present as people on the bus shouted, "Stop! Halt!" Their grinning driver, however, drove blithely past the group of wildly waving tourists at the bus stop, then stopped at the next. There seemed neither rhyme nor reason to his stops, and many of the passengers on the bus finally laughed with the driver, caught up in the spirit of a wild escapade. Paula smiled hopelessly with the others at their unlikely ride.

Suddenly Vanessa stood. "Matt, isn't this the bridge where we get off?"

"Yes, of course! But I'd told him . . ." By the time Matt explained to the bus driver, several long blocks had passed.

"We'll have to walk all the way back to the bridge," Vanessa complained, intertwining her arm with Matt's. "Your wonderful Spanish at work, I presume?"

Matt laughed, extending his other arm to Paula, and she managed a pleasant smile as she took it. She decided again that he was trying to create an atmosphere in which all three of them would be comfortable. It reminded her all too much of Tony's balancing acts between women.

When they arrived on the dusty path under the causeway bridge, twenty or so other tourists were waiting to catch the nine-thirty boat. Within minutes a Mexican official arrived. "Today we have unusual circumstances," he explained. "The nine-thirty boat to Isla Mujeres goes at eleven-thirty."

The crowd was furious.

"No sense in letting it ruin our day," Paula finally said.

Vanessa ignored her. "If only we'd chartered our own boat!"

Matt raised a warning brow. "A little adversity is good for acquiring the virtue of patience," he commented. "Now let's see that beautiful smile, Vanessa."

Vanessa put on a spurious smile.

After wandering through the gift shops of the nearby hotels, they sat out on the white sandy beach facing the distant island of Isla Mujeres.

"So close, and yet so far," Matt said ironically as they watched the fishing boats, yachts, and sightseeing boats cut through the sparkling water.

"Nothing is lost on a writer," Paula replied, making notes about the varicolored sea with its striations of purple and great luminous streaks of turquoise. "It's so beautiful that I'd be happy just to sit here all day."

The truth, much as she fought it, was that she would be happy to be anywhere with Matt. She hoped that her feeling wasn't obvious. It was a pleasure to glance occasionally at him. He didn't seem too engrossed in his paperback novel, and her heart leapt hopefully as he looked at her.

"Good book?" she inquired with a glance at his paperback.

"Not bad," he answered.

She suspected that the book was irrelevant to their interchange. Yet there seemed nothing of consequence to discuss with Vanessa on the other side of him, and Paula tried to block out the inner voice that repeated over and over: *He's attracted to both of you!*

Just after eleven o'clock they all made their way back to the boat dock under the bridge. A throng of tourists waited, perhaps a hundred, nearly all of them grumbling about the boat's delay. Apparently an insurance convention group had chartered the scheduled boat out from under them.

"Just the sort of thing to expect," Vanessa remarked.

Finally their boat was sighted in the channel, and soon they were boarding. "Free drinks down below," the woman in charge said to counter the loud complaints.

Later, Paula sat out on the deck of the boat gratefully sipping a cool cola and admiring the view as they cut through the brilliant sea. The beauty of the pale blue sky and the shimmering water made the day dreamlike. Then she glanced beside her at Matt and saw Vanessa's hand on his shoulder.

The woman's amber eyes danced with secrets as she talked to him. It was impossible to imagine what Matt was thinking behind his dark glasses, but he most definitely seemed interested in what Vanessa had to say.

Paula contemplated a new idea. Was it possible that he loved both of them in different ways? Certainly she and Vanessa provided the variety to amuse a playboy: Vanessa, the sophisticated jet setter; Paula, the innocent girl next door who adored him. The more she considered the notion, the more certain she became of its truth. Matt enjoyed dangling two women, just as Tony had! Why hadn't she seen it immediately? Why didn't she learn?

Yet I promised to wait and see, to give the situation this last day! she reminded herself. She glanced again at Matt and Vanessa. Vanessa caught Matt's face in her hands and playfully kissed his cheek.

Paula turned away in shock. His face had been averted and she hadn't seen his expression, but he certainly wasn't resisting just then!

She was hurt, then enraged with herself as well as with them. Enough! She'd given him the benefit of the doubt over and over; she'd given him enough of this last day already too. Never again would she play this threesome game. She'd be polite to Matt, but nothing else.

As they approached the weatherbeaten docks at Isla Mujeres, Paula jotted notes, despite her shredded emotions. *Turquoise sea, white sandy beach, palm trees and thatch-roofed ramadas climbing the hillside, tourists everywhere*. She saw that Matt had finally extricated himself from Vanessa and was taking pictures of the tropical island scene.

The woman managing the boat announced to her passengers, "Because of complications this morning, we are running two hours late. We cannot pick you up until five-thirty; then we'll take you to dinner on the other end of the island—"

198

"We'll be lucky to get back by night!" Vanessa protested into the general anger voiced by the passengers.

Paula decided not to worry about it. It appeared that all she'd need tonight was packing time anyhow! She'd leave a farewell note at the hotel desk for Matt tomorrow morning, she thought, pretending that her heart didn't ache.

Matt and Vanessa waited on the dock. What a peculiar threesome they must make, Paula thought resentfully as she joined them. They strolled along, surveying the sights; watery pens along the dock holding enormous turtles, grizzled fishermen extracting meat from huge conch shells, tourists snorkeling in the foaming surf.

After browsing through the colorful outdoor shops Matt suggested, "Why don't we have lunch and then spend the afternoon on the beach?"

How could he appear so innocent? Paula fumed.

"It doesn't look as if there's anything else to do here," Vanessa answered. "If only we'd chartered a boat!"

Matt cast her a warning glance. "No one forced you to come here."

Vanessa blanched, looking taken aback. "I'm sorry."

"Forget it," Matt replied.

At least Vanessa's complaining *did* bother him, Paula decided with a touch of vengeance.

"Now who else is starved?" he asked.

"I'm famished," Paula answered, not adding that being upset made her hungry.

"Wonderful!" he said.

As they climbed the sandy hillside to the restaurant, Vanessa seemed intent on winning her way back into Matt's favor. "It is lovely," she was saying, then adding something about being so happy she'd come.

Was Matt such a fool that he might be taken in by the

woman's sudden reversal? Paula wondered. It didn't seem possible.

Paula entered the outdoor restaurant just in front of them. Behind her, Vanessa took Matt's arm, and Paula felt obliged to follow the maître d' to their table at the wooden railing overlooking the sea. The man no doubt assumed that Matt and Vanessa were a couple, and seated them together across the table.

Paula's anger grew as Vanessa deferred to Matt, hanging on his every word. At first it seemed an act, but then Vanessa seemed serious. Perhaps she needed a man to approve of her because she'd had no father around during her childhood. Perhaps she was suddenly afraid of displeasing Matt.

Gayle had warned her in Merida, "You have to fight for him." But how? She most certainly was not going to throw herself into Matt's arms! If he didn't like her for herself and preferred Vanessa, there was no help for it. Perhaps there never had been.

After they'd ordered their lunches, Paula tried to control her emotions. Matt was taking pictures of the magnificent seaside views, and she pulled out her notebook, supposing she'd have to write something. *Isla Mujeres is an idyllic island,* she jotted unenthusiastically. *A coconut palm covered sand bar.* She speculated on what a tourbook might call the white beaches; perhaps "unexcelled." Part of her heartbreak, she thought, was that it was so beautiful here, she should be enjoying it, not feeling so miserable.

Her lunch of salad and turtle soup was delicious, but Vanessa monopolized Matt, excluding Paula from the conversation about Cozumel so completely that it was impossible to enjoy anything. According to Vanessa, the photographic possibilities at Cozumel were nothing less than sensational. Occasionally Matt tried to include Paula, but she was so uncomfortable that her words seemed contrived, as if another person spoke through her lips.

When she'd finished her lunch, she wrote in her notebook to conceal her anguish. After a while she looked around the room and noticed the three couples from the bus stop in Cancun sitting at a nearby table.

One of the women smiled at her. "Would any of you like to hire a taxi with us to drive out to the ruin on the south end of the island? The six of us don't quite fill two taxis."

Paula glanced at Matt and Vanessa. It sounded as if they were planning to leave for Cozumel anyhow! Rising from the table Paula excused herself. "I think I'll go with them . . . ," she began with a catch in her throat.

Caught up in the conversation, Matt nodded.

More hurt than ever, Paula stopped at the other table. "Thank you, I'd like to share a taxi with you if I may. I'll wait in front of the restaurant."

"We'll be with you in a minute," the woman said.

Outside, Paula sat down dully on a wooden bench. Blinking to hold back her tears, she tried to concentrate on the sea. Moments later, the three couples joined her, introducing themselves as they all walked to the road where local taxis waited. Her new companions were a jolly, enthusiastic group. Perhaps some of their attitude would rub off on her, Paula hoped, as they split up into the taxis.

It was a relief to escape the continual tension of being with Matt and Vanessa as the taxis bounced along to the south end of the island. The wives and husbands in the group seemed so congenial, getting along together, and with the others too. Why couldn't she find someone to love like that?

They piled out of the two taxis near a small Mayan ruin overlooking the shimmering sea. The Temple of Ix Chel seemed mere rubble compared to the ruins they had already seen. It was nothing at all like Uxmal, Kabah, Chichen Itza, or Tulum, yet it was a remnant of the glory of the Mayans too.

According to her guidebook it had probably been a coastal stop for the ancient Mayans during their religious processions. The text said, *When the Spaniards first landed on Isla Mujeres in 1517, there were hundreds of clay statues to Ix Chel, the goddess of fertility. Thus they named the place Island of Women.*

A place for women who wanted children. Women like her, whose dream it was to have a happy family, Paula thought. Maybe it was best that her loving Matt had proved futile. He'd never want children. He wanted to travel, to photograph places and people. There was no place for a wife in his life, except for a jet setter like Vanessa, who probably didn't want children either.

When everyone returned to the taxis, hers had a flat tire. Another of Gayle's blessings in disguise? Paula wondered bitterly. Sitting down on a rock, she pulled out her notebook. If nothing else, she could work on her article and on her tan. It would be hours until the boat's return.

By the time their driver came back with a new tire, changed it, and drove her group to the beach area, it was after four o'clock.

Paula walked out to the beach, even more heartsick when she spotted Matt and Vanessa. Sunburned, they were lying on lounges in the shade of a ramada. She reluctantly made her way down to them.

"Where on earth have you been?" Matt asked as he rose to his feet.

Bewildered by his agitation, she explained, "To Ix Chel, the Mayan ruin—"

"I thought you'd left for the restroom! And then when you didn't return . . ."

202

If you hadn't been so intrigued with Vanessa and her spiel about Cozumel, you might have heard me! she thought. She said instead, "I did tell you I was going with the three couples from the bus stop."

"I'm sorry, I must not have heard," he apologized, looking appalled. "Is there time for me to go to get pictures of the ruins?"

Vanessa's amber eyes flashed with irritation. "Now? The boat should pick us up in an hour!"

"There's no need for photographs," Paula said. "It's a very minor ruin, nothing compared to what we've seen." She looked around. "Where is everyone?" Only a few visitors lolled in the sun, and most of them were already sunburned.

"Some of them came by chartered boats and they've already left," Vanessa said, pouting. "Not to mention the insurance group who chartered our boat away from us. It came by for them at three-thirty."

Matt added, "Some of our group have taken taxis to town and are going back to Cancun on the ferry. There's still plenty of time for our boat to come."

For a moment Paula thought she might lie out on the beach to avoid the torment of being with them, but her arms and legs were already red, as were her shoulders. She settled at a nearby wooden table in the shade of a ramada and produced her notebook again. "I'm going to try to finish the article," she announced as much to herself as to them.

She never became quite oblivious to them as she wrote. Vanessa seemed to sleep, and Matt was reading. The breeze cooled Paula's sunburn and the sound of the sea lulled her churning emotions. She would fly home tomorrow morning without fail.

At five-thirty she had finished the first draft of her article. Looking up, she saw no sign of their boat on the shimmering sea, only occasional fishing boats returning to the other end of Isla Mujeres.

The couples with whom she'd shared the taxi hurried up the nearby path. "We're going to take taxis to the ferry," one of the men explained. "The last ferry today leaves at six-thirty!"

"The *last* ferry?" Paula repeated, putting away her note-book. "I'd like to go with you!" She didn't dare get marooned for the night on the island if she were to catch the morning plane home!

"Maybe we'd better go too," Matt suggested, getting to his feet.

"On the local ferry?" Vanessa asked, aghast. "And how will we get to our hotels?"

"There are supposed to be taxis on the other end," the man replied.

Other stragglers on the beach seemed to make the same decision at once, and everyone jammed into the few roadside taxis.

On the crowded old ferry, Paula found one of the last seats on the top deck among the natives and crates of chickens, grateful at least that she had a place to sit. Watching the magnificent sunset, she attempted to excise her anguish although she knew full well that Matt and Vanessa leaned on the railing far behind her. Out of sight, out of mind, she tried to tell herself, but it wasn't working.

As the last lingering rays of light hung over the sea, Paula found herself turning to look at them against the railing. Vanessa was reaching up to Matt, then kissing him.

Paula twisted away. Fool! How could she have been so stupid and blind to have fallen for him again? His interest in her had been a mirage, an illusion. This was reality!

Night had fallen when the ferry docked. Shaking with

emótion, Paula made her way off the ship and peered out into the darkness. There was no sign of taxis, no lights of a city. Old trucks and cars roared off the ferry beside her as she made her way along the rutted roadside. In the middle of nowhere . . . how appropriate!

"Paula!" Matt called. "Over here. There's only a bus."

A truck's lights illuminated the night for a moment, and she saw Matt and Vanessa running for a battered bus.

Another truck roared toward her, but she crossed in front of it. Brakes screeched and a horn honked angrily.

"You might have been killed!" Matt exclaimed as he let her onto the bus in front of him.

She didn't care, she was tempted to say. She didn't even care!

The battered bus was jammed; natives had already gathered up their children onto their laps, but the spaces were quickly filled. The bus driver closed the door despite the long line of passengers waiting in the darkness.

"Paula?" It was one of the women with whom she'd shared the taxi to Ix Chel. "Maybe you can squeeze in here."

"Thanks," she said gratefully. She perched on the edge of a double seat already crowded with the American as well as a Mexican woman and baby.

The American woman said, "I know you've been sick. You're probably pale under that sunburn."

It wouldn't be surprising, Paula thought, hanging onto the railing as the bus took off and bounced through the darkness. She looked around for Matt and Vanessa, and might have laughed if she weren't so heartsick.

Vanessa, looking furious, stood with a Mexican woman within the rusty chrome rim of what had once been a seat. Matt was jammed in the crowd standing at the rear of the bus.

The ride seemed interminable, made bearable only by the

gurgling infant in the smiling Mexican woman's arms. Outside the world was dark, and Paula imagined the low growing trees and tangled undergrowth of jungle. It suddenly struck her that the bus might not be going where they thought. "Cancun?" she asked the woman.

She nodded, pleased to be helpful. "Sí, Cancun."

When lights did appear, it was another city. Puerto Juarez. The bus stopped and locals disembarked, only to be replaced by American tourists who'd been left behind at the ferry. "We hitched a ride on a pickup truck," one of them explained. Laughter filled the bus as the tourists compared notes.

"What a fiasco," the American woman beside Paula chuckled. "An elegant vacation in Cancun, and they're riding through the night in the jungle on a pickup truck!"

Paula forced a smile. "Not quite what the tourist brochures advertise, is it?"

Finally the bus stopped in downtown Cancun, and Paula disembarked with the other tourists. Matt joined the line of men flagging down taxis.

He held the rear door open for her. "You look awfully tired. I hope the day wasn't too much for you."

"I'll no doubt live," she replied.

Vanessa sat in the middle beside her, and Paula lay her head back on the top of the seat, closing her eyes. None of them spoke as they rode back to the hotel. An exhausting day for everyone, Paula thought, trying desperately not to recall the image of Vanessa kissing him.

At the hotel, she rushed for the elevator, not caring whether they followed. When she stepped on, they were right behind her.

"Are you feeling worse, Paula?" Matt inquired. "You're so quiet."

"I'll be fine." She wondered if she would really ever be fine

206

again. In any case, she would shower, call the airlines, and finish packing.

His blue eyes watched her intently. "How about dinner?"

"No thanks, I'm not hungry—just tired."

"But you have to eat."

Her temper flared. "I just want to be alone!"

His eyes widened as he backed away. "Sorry."

Behind him, Vanessa smiled triumphantly.

When the elevator door opened, Paula rushed through the corridor for her room.

In her room, she pulled off her clothing and stepped into the shower, letting the spray of lukewarm water cleanse her and soothe her sunburn, if not her agony.

By the time she stepped out, she felt as if she might survive. She slipped into her embroidered caftan and telephoned room service for a cup of soup, and the airport to make arrangements. It was better not to think, she decided as she began to pack furiously. She'd spent too much of her life thinking about Matt, tormenting herself over him. She'd made a mess, nearly throwing him into Vanessa's arms, but then he hadn't required much urging either.

She found the coral necklace and earrings that Evan had given her. She would send him a check. She remembered him drunkenly rushing at her and turned the memory away. Ashes. Everything about her and men disintegrated into ashes. She'd run away from Tony only to slam into the confrontation with Evan—and heartbreak with Matt! Never, never again!

She turned, seeing her grief reflected in the mirror and quite suddenly a sob escaped, then another and another.

You're only feeling sorry for yourself, an inner voice murmured through her despair.

And who else would feel sorry for me? she returned with angry sobs. *I could drop dead in this hotel and not one person here would care, not one!*

She threw herself on the bed, sobbing uncontrollably. If God loved her the way that Gayle said, then why did she have to endure heartache with men over and over? Why had she even been born? What was the purpose of life?

It was a long time before she sat up and wiped her eyes. Trembling with wretchedness, she supposed Gayle would say something again about having to give your whole life over to Jesus, that it wasn't enough just to pray occasionally. "I don't think you've ever committed yourself *unreservedly* to Jesus," Gayle had said. *"Unreservedly."*

Gayle said she'd been angry with God when her father died, and Paula knew that she was mad at Him now too. It was unfair! Unfair that no man loved her, and that Matt—whom she'd loved for so many years—preferred a woman like Vanessa! If God was so good, why wasn't he fair too?

She recalled Gayle saying that no one had promised that life would be fair . . . or what we might think is fair. And then Gayle had spoken on Christ, who strengthened her.

Tearfully, Paula mulled it over. It was true that she'd never surrendered *everything* to God. She'd never surrendered *anything,* and right now, there was nothing to surrender!

"All right, I surrender!" she cried out hopelessly. "I give up everything to you! I've made a mess of my life anyhow. If it is true that Jesus died for me and my sins, I would really like to know," she continued. "I would so like to straighten my life around, to find the joy and peace with Jesus that Gayle talks about." An enormous sob escaped her lips and she fell onto her knees.

After a moment, she realized that she *had* meant every word of it. She was tired of trying to manage on her own, tired of hurting over Tony and Evan and—Matt. "But if only you'd give me someone to love, someone who'd love me too. . . ."

Paula felt a sudden glow in her heart as if a lamp had been lit. The golden warmth spread rapidly through her and joy leapt in her soul. Waves of love swept through her like torrents until she was surrounded and permeated by what could only be God's embrace.

I love you! I love you! her soul responded. *I just didn't know. . . .*

It might have been an eternity or merely moments before she opened her eyes. She only knew that an amazing joy had filled her soul. With such happiness, she thought, it didn't matter if she never had a man to love her. If it was God's will for her to be single forever, then it really didn't matter. Nothing else mattered now. She felt healed and cleansed— reborn with love. How astonishing that she had come to the Yucatan to see the religious sites of a pagan people—ancients who had sacrificed live children to their bloodthirsty gods— and that she had found a loving God instead.

For a long time she could only marvel at what had happened to her. Finally, her thoughts returned to her surroundings, to her situation, and she was reminded of Vanessa. To Paula's amazement, she found her heart filling with compassion and love for the woman; it was as if she could see the unhappy child in Vanessa—the immature girl who'd never grown up. Surely, only God's love could make her feel such sudden tenderness for someone so difficult to love.

A knock sounded at her door. "Room service," the accented voice announced.

Still caught up in wonder, she opened the door.

The young Mexican bellboy nodded politely and carried her tray across the room, flipped on the dining room light, and arranged her soup and crackers. Collecting her wits, she found her purse and a tip for him. She recalled the doctor's parting words and said, "*Vaya con Dios.* Go with God."

"Gracias," the bellboy replied with a surprised smile, then headed for the open doorway.

Matt stood at the door, with an armful of roses. "I was hoping to talk to you, Paula."

Stunned, she gazed at him. For a dreamlike moment it seemed that they were in another time and place—by his front steps with the sunshine streaming down through the trees.

"Come in," she offered hesitantly.

"I hardly know what to say," he began, "only that I made such a mistake, letting you go."

"No, Matt! Not again!"

"Please hear me out," he asked. "And please accept the roses."

As she took them, she realized that there were red, yellow, pink, and white roses jumbled together—much like the armful she'd brought to him that Saturday morning over two years ago. "Thank you," she said with a catch in her voice. She looked into his eyes and seemed to see into his soul.

His words were contrite. "That morning you brought me the roses, it was as if God stopped the world for an instant and said, 'Look at this lovely girl who's all grown up now.'"

He smiled nervously, then continued. "I knew that there was something special about the feeling, and about you. But I just wasn't ready. I was still power hungry, money hungry. I knew you were a nice young woman, that it wouldn't just be a few kisses and all over. You have no idea how I struggled against reaching for your hand that night when we went to a movie, against taking you into my arms at your front door."

"And I thought you saw me as a little sister—"

"No . . . not since that morning of the roses. It seemed as if it were a moment caught in time. And then I fell off that old kitchen stool into your arms. If ever God shoved anyone!"

"God?" she inquired. The first time he'd mentioned Him could have been something anyone might have said, but now—a second time. "I've never really heard you mention God since you were a boy speaking in church. I thought you'd given up on Him."

Matt shook his head. "I did for a long time, but—well, I told you and Josh that you didn't really know me anymore. Something happened to me several months ago. You see, I'd come to such a low after selling the company—when I should have been soaring with happiness. After it sold, I felt so useless, so directionless. Worse, I was besieged with 'new friends' who were interested in my money. Everything seemed futile. Finally I thought back to the most joyous moments of my life."

"And . . . ?"

"I remembered when I'd been close to the Lord as a boy." He paused self-consciously, then went on. "I finally got down on my knees and asked if he'd have me back, despite my turning away."

"And did he?" Paula asked hopefully.

Matt nodded. "It seems he's always waiting for us."

"He was waiting for me too," she said with a surge of joy. For a moment they reveled in the happiness of each other's eyes, then a horrid thought invaded her mind. What if she'd misunderstood? What if he were only leading up to Vanessa, the woman he'd always loved? It was better to say it herself: "And now God's returned Vanessa to your life!"

"Vanessa?" he asked, his brow furrowing. "Yes, I suppose so, though she was the last person I expected to see again."

"You certainly didn't flee," Paula pointed out.

Matt nodded. "I couldn't help being flattered to see her chasing me after—after dumping me for an older man with money. She admitted she'd made a bad mistake, giving me up.

So, when I thought you preferred Evan, I wanted to see if there was still anything between Vanessa and me."

He paused for a long time, and Paula remembered Matt and Vanessa kissing on the dance floor in Merida and tonight at the railing of the ferry.

"There's nothing left," he said. "I began to suspect it when she insisted on going on that calesa ride in Merida. She threw herself at me, but I was in no mood to catch her."

"I don't understand. . . ."

"Vanessa and I have grown in opposite directions. It would never work again."

"But you kissed her tonight on the ferry!" Paula protested.

Matt shook his head. "No," he said. "I phoned her in Cozumel to tell her it was all over."

"But you two were kissing on the boat and on the ferry!"

"Vanessa doesn't give up easily," Matt explained. "She saw you look toward us. *She* kissed *me*. It was the same sort of kiss she forced me into on the dance floor in Merida. I'm afraid she staged them, in part, to make you mad at me."

"Vanessa hoped to make *me* mad at you?" Paula asked.

He nodded. "You see, after you disappeared this afternoon, I was so upset that I told her I love you."

Paula blinked in amazement. "That you love me?"

"That I love you," he replied solemnly. "And when we returned to the hotel and you dashed off into the elevator so mad, I thought that maybe . . . just maybe you loved me too."

"Oh, Matt!" How did he *not* know that she'd loved him all this time? Could she have possibly kept it so well hidden?

His blue eyes brimmed with love. "Please marry me, Paula?"

Overwhelmed, she didn't know what to say. She'd dreamed for years of this moment, but now . . . now obstacles loomed. For one, her jealousy. After what she'd just gone through with Vanessa, she couldn't bear to endure it again. Women would always chase after him. "But, Matt," she protested, "even your mother says you're a playboy."

"A playboy?" he asked, astonished. After a moment, understanding flashed in his eyes. "I suppose it's because she's from another generation. Her meaning of the word isn't quite what it's taken for nowadays. If anything, my fault was being a workaholic. But I know what I'll be vowing to God about forsaking all others. I'm ready to settle down, Paula. And I want to settle down with you. I want you to have our children."

"Children? But I thought that you wanted to travel, to photograph the world!"

"Only if I can do it with you," he responded, "and not all of the time. There'd be summer vacations and years later when the children are grown. There would be so much else to do in our own little world, a lifetime of pictures to take!"

They looked into each other's eyes over the roses, then he took them from her, placing them on the dresser at their side. "I love you so much," he murmured.

"And I've always loved you, ever since I was a little girl."

"Then will you marry me?"

"Yes, Matt . . . oh, yes."

When their lips met she forgot everything except that her greatest wish had come true, that God had given her this wonderful man, that he had been meant for her.

When they moved away to catch their breath, she suddenly remembered. "But I'm flying home tomorrow morning!"

"Not without me," he said huskily, then smiled. "And I hope we're not going to have to wait until June for the wedding. We've known each other quite a while."

"We could get married here, I suppose."

"But I'd like to have your parents' blessing," he said firmly.

Surely he would have it if he told them about what had happened to him. God would work that out too.

"Don't you want a church wedding?" Matt asked.

"Yes, I really do!" In her mind's eye she could already visualize it in the neighborhood church where she'd seen him speak so many years ago, where she'd sung hymns before she'd had the vaguest inkling about God's love and joy.

Matt dropped a kiss on her forehead, then glanced at the dining area. "We can't have soup and crackers for our engagement dinner!" he said with a laugh. "Besides, it's probably a good idea for us to go downstairs for dinner."

Paula felt herself blushing, then loving him all the more.

As she gathered up her purse and room key she thought she might be floating. *Thank you! Oh, thank you!* she prayed joyously. She recalled again the golden warmth that had spread rapidly through her, and it seemed that Matt's love had followed like an echo. It was as if God had shown how much he loved them, and that they were to reflect it, to spend their lifetimes on earth echoing and reechoing his love.

ABOUT THE AUTHOR

ELAINE SCHULTE was born and raised in Crown Point, Indiana, and graduated from Purdue University, which recently honored her with a "Distinguished Alumna" award. She has written hundreds of short stories, general articles, and travel articles that have appeared in magazines and newspapers around the world. One of her novels often appears on television.

Echoes of Love is Schulte's second contemporary romance novel for Zondervan; her first, *On Wings of Love,* launched Serenade Books in 1983. *Song of Joy,* her third contemporary, will be published in early 1987.

Her two historical novels, *Westward My Love* and its sequel *Dreams of Gold,* were published earlier this year.

Schulte lived in Belgium for several years and has traveled extensively in Europe, the Middle East, Africa, and North America. She and her husband live in Rancho Santa Fe, California. They have two sons.

A Letter to Our Readers

Dear Reader:

Welcome to Serenade Books—a series designed to bring you beautiful love stories in the world of inspirational romance. They will uplift you, encourage you, and provide hours of wholesome entertainment, so thousands of readers have testified. That we might better contribute to your reading enjoyment, we would appreciate your taking a few minutes to respond to the following questions and return to:

> Lois Taylor
> Serenade Books
> The Zondervan Publishing House
> 1415 Lake Drive, S.E.
> Grand Rapids, Michigan 49506

1. Did you enjoy reading ECHOES OF LOVE?

   ☐ Very much. I would like to see more books by this author!
   ☐ Moderately
   ☐ I would have enjoyed it more if _____

2. Where did you purchase this book? _____

3. What influenced your decision to purchase this book?

   ☐ Cover   ☐ Back cover copy
   ☐ Title   ☐ Friends
   ☐ Publicity   ☐ Other _____

4. Please rate the following elements from 1 (poor) to 10 (superior).

☐ Heroine   ☐ Plot
☐ Hero   ☐ Inspirational theme
☐ Setting   ☐ Secondary characters

5. What are some inspirational themes you would like to see treated in future books?

_____

_____

6. Please indicate your age range:

☐ Under 18   ☐ 25–34   ☐ 46–55
☐ 18–24   ☐ 35–45   ☐ Over 55

Serenade / Saga books are inspirational romances in historical settings, designed to bring you a joyful, heart-lifting reading experience.

Serenade / Saga books available in your local bookstore:

Serenade / Serenata books are inspirational romances in contemporary settings, designed to bring you a joyful, heartlifting reading experience.

#25 *One More River*, Suzanne Pierson Ellison
#26 *Journey Toward Tomorrow*, Karyn Carr
#27 *Flower of the Sea*, Amanda Clark
#28 *Shadows Along the Ice*, Judy Baer
#29 *Born to Be One*, Cathie LeNoir
#30 *Heart Aflame*, Susan Kirby
#31 *By Love Restored*, Nancy Johanson
#32 *Karaleen*, Mary Carpenter Reid
#33 *Love's Full Circle*, Lurlene McDaniel
#34 *A New Love*, Mab Graff Hoover
#35 *The Lessons of Love*, Susan Phillips
#36 *For Always*, Molly Noble Bull
#37 *A Song in the Night*, Sara Mitchell
#38 *Love Unmerited*, Donna Fletcher Crow
#39 *Thetis Island*, Brenda Willoughby
#40 *Love More Precious*, Marilyn Austin

Watch for other books in both the *Serenade/Saga* (historical) and *Serenade/Serenata* (contemporary) series, coming soon.

Date Due